L.A. Confrontational

PETE DAVID

Published by Hawkpoint Press

ISBN:10: 0692373853
ISBN-13: 978-0-692-37385-9

ACKNOWLEDGMENTS

Thanks to my writer's critique group members, Bob Kidera, Susan (Wrona) Gall, Terry Civello, and Ann Hartung for their thorough review of multiple drafts.

I am grateful to my editors, Eliza Stevens and Lisa McCoy, for their suggestions and attention to detail. As always, my sister, Jennifer Sheehan, provided an early reading and excellent input. My Florida agent Ron Bearzotti provided invaluable comments on an early draft.

Thanks to Officer Michael De La Hunt of the LAPD and Lieutenant Pete Golden of the Bernalillo County Sheriff's Department for allowing me to pick their brains about local law enforcement issues. Jack Zipper contributed additional guidance on weapons and accessories.

The cover design was provided by the talented artist, Angela Farinelli.

Thank you Carolyn for your love and support.

CHAPTER 1

Mrs. Bennett leaned forward, providing me with an ample view of the fleshy chasm above her low-cut dress. I accepted her check and pretended not to notice. She'd become friendlier with each piece of evidence documenting her husband's affair with a female bartender.

A month earlier, she had collapsed in tears at the prospect of losing her 15-year marriage. "What am I going to do now?"

"Look, Mrs. Bennett. My evidence will get you a nice alimony payment. My recommendation is to take the money and go on a nice vacation. There's nothing better than a gondola trip down a Venice canal to help you forget your problems." The suggestion was strictly for my client's benefit. I didn't follow my own advice.

The large number of divorce cases I accepted to pay the bills prompted me to understand the factors contributing to marriage failure. The reasons mine fizzled were obvious and I had spent the previous year fighting the demons that followed me from my six-year stint with the Los Angeles Police Department. I had hoped to find either peace or prosperity. I'm not greedy. I would have been content with one out of two.

I wished Mrs. Bennett luck while ushering her out the door. The thing about luck: it's either random or non-existent. Like the case of the rich guy who wins the lottery—luck and fairness are complete strangers. Sure, they say money can't buy happiness, but being affluent opens doors, and at the moment I was encountering numerous locked ones. It had been tough making a living in Albuquerque.

The square plastic clock on my wall read 10:00 am. No more appointments scheduled for today. I held out my hand parallel with the top of my second-hand credenza desk. The slight tremor came from lack of coffee. As I contemplated heading out for a jolt of java, a well-dressed man appeared at my office doorway.

Frank Minor's entry into my life didn't bring me luck, but his job offer turned my tedious life upside down.

I gave him an inquisitive nod of my head. "Can I help you?"

He stared at me as if trying to make up his mind. "Are you Arch Caldwell?" He asked in a deep, firm voice.

"Yes. Come in and have a seat." I motioned to the lone red velvet club chair across from my desk.

The man's blond hair was short and neat. He wore a dark blue suit, white shirt, and multi-colored tie. His thin middle-aged frame extended beyond my six feet. From the clothing design, he looked like money. Maybe. Expensive designer duds can be purchased for next to nothing at any number of thrift shops around the city.

"Frank Minor. Call me Frank." We shook hands across the desk.

"Nice to meet you, Frank. Did you ever play basketball?"

"No, I wasn't very good at basketball. Volleyball was my sport. You look like you could play some ball."

My youthful appearance probably surprised him, a frequent reaction when first-time clients met me, assuming I was considerably older based on my phone voice and conversation. A few even admitted they preferred someone with more experience. "I played football in college. I try to keep in shape, but it does get harder as we get older." My explanation didn't appear to convince him to hire me. I often spent more time trying to keep clients than working for them, especially those impatient with my progress. Why were people in such a hurry to get bad news?

He glanced at the walls as if looking for some kind of diploma or other reassurance about his decision to request my services. He finally looked back at me. "I got your name from Jimmy Klaussen, the manager at Flying Star. He said you were discreet."

"Well, you can't always believe what Jimmy says, but he got that part right. What can I do for you?"

"I want you to find my daughter." He reached into a large envelope and slid across my desk an 8 x 10 color photo of a pretty, teenage girl wearing a purple wool skirt and matching jacket over a white top.

"Let's start with her name."

"Sarah."

"How recent is this photo?"

"It was taken on her sixteenth birthday, last year. She turned seventeen last month."

"How long has she been missing?"

Frank hesitated. "I haven't seen her in six months. She left my house in Rio Rancho and never came back."

I leaned back in my chair. "Six months? Why did you wait so long?"

"It's complicated. Her mother and I were going through a divorce and I hired a private detective, and...things didn't work out so well. We were pursuing a joint custody agreement at the time." He stopped and seemed to be considering whether to tell me more.

A cup of hot coffee was calling my name, but I needed this case. "You want to elaborate, Frank?" I reached over and grabbed my small spiral notebook and a Dodgers pen, hoping the deliberate activity would convince him to provide more information.

"The PI got emotionally involved in the case."

I looked at the photo again. The blossoming beauty in her cheekbones and warm eyes was evident. "I see. You mean romantically?"

"Yes, but not with my daughter." He sighed and looked at the ceiling.

"Frank, I need you to level with me if we're going to have a successful relationship and find Sarah. Jimmy told you I was discreet. Your information is confidential. It will not be divulged to anyone, unless it's absolutely necessary to keep my ass out of jail."

"He started dating my ex-wife." He said it casually, with no real emotion.

"While the divorce was pending?"

"Yes, we were separated."

"I see. I'll need the name of the PI and your wife. Where is she now?"

"In Santa Fe. She's reverted to her maiden name, Carson. Barbara Carson. I put together a summary to help you with the case." He reached inside the envelope and handed me several sheets of paper on stationary belonging to the Castor, Minor and Kaplansky law firm.

The information included a chronological list of events. The final page contained names and contact info, including one very familiar name.

"Andy Lujan? He was the PI you hired?"

"Yes. I figured you might know him."

"I know Andy. The PIs in this town are a close community." Andy had been a good friend, occasional mentor, and a business competitor the past year. I met him in California, and he helped me when I fled Los Angeles. "Is Andy still on the payroll?"

"No, I stopped paying him a few months ago and haven't heard from him since. As far as I know, Barbara, my ex, stopped seeing him, or perhaps it was the other way around. I didn't trust he would be committed to the case."

"How long have you and your wife been separated?"

"Almost two years. I included Barb's contact info. And information on a few of Sarah's friends."

"Do you know if Sarah had any enemies? Or maybe an abusive boyfriend?"

"I can't think of anyone who would want to harm her."

"Was she attending school?"

"Yes, she was at Santa Fe High School."

"I take it this is your law firm?" I pointed to the logo at the top of the first page.

"Yes, we do real estate law. Will you take the case?"

I studied Frank. He probably had some money, but who had a lot these days? I rarely got a client rich enough to let me get away with raising my rates. I figured he could afford my standard rates of one-fifty a day plus expenses. It wasn't going to make me rich, but in a small market like Albuquerque, the rates had to be competitive. Andy's rates were higher, but he had more experience. I needed the income.

Frank produced a personal check in response to my requirement of a five hundred dollar retainer fee. I pulled up the contract form on my laptop, filled in the pertinent info, and handed him the two printed copies.

He spent a few minutes reading the contract before reaching for a pen out of my Lakers cup and signing. He returned one signed copy to me.

I slipped the contract into a folder. "What's the best way to communicate with you?"

Frank pulled his law firm business card from his wallet. "Please don't contact me at work. I'm giving you my personal cell phone number." He wrote the number on the card, and handed it to me.

"Okay, Frank. Anything else you'd like to tell me that might not be included in your summary? Could Sarah just be hanging out in Santa Fe with your ex?"

"Barbara insists she hasn't seen Sarah in at least six months. We're both upset, and of course the ex blames me for everything. I'm worried about Sarah, especially given all those young women found dead on the mesa."

Frank referred to a famous cold case in Albuquerque, the discovery on the West Mesa of the remains of eleven women, thought to be prostitutes. Having worked vice at the LAPD, I knew a lot about hookers. "Those bodies were discovered nearly four years ago."

"Sarah's disappearance made me think of the case."

"Do you believe she's turning tricks?"

Frank's face paled. "I can't imagine her being a prostitute."

"I have to ask. We can't rule it out, especially if she hasn't been in contact with anyone. What about drug use?"

"She smoked pot. I confronted her when she stayed with me during the summer school break." Dismay spread across Frank's face. "The next morning she left the house and never returned."

I looked again at his list. The address for his ex-wife was on Canyon Road, a winding narrow street filled with art galleries and small shops. "I'll start with a visit to Barbara. Is she an artist?"

"Yes. She owns a small art gallery. It's not always open, but she's usually working in the studio. There's an entrance door on the right side of the building."

"All right, Frank. I'll need to contact Andy to see what he's got on the case. I'll keep you updated on my progress."

"Thank you." We shook hands. His palms were sweaty despite the coolness in the office.

After Frank left, I jotted down some case notes on my laptop. I studied the photo on my desk of my ex-wife and daughter. Joanne had scolded me repeatedly about not being responsible enough in raising Josie. Of course, that wasn't the only reason why she left me.

Being married to an L.A. cop was a tough sentence in itself, even before the scandal hit and I took my professional nosedive.

I locked the office door and went downstairs to the small diner owned and operated by Bud Steiner. Bud must have been in his early sixties, and had named the diner Bud's. I always liked to kid him that Steiner's Finer Diner had a nice ring to it.

After I helped his oldest son through a nasty divorce case, Bud offered to lease me the small office. He never pursued me for the rent, but I tried to pay him something when possible. The strong smell of bacon had seeped into my office, and I needed to leave before my clothes reeked like the restaurant.

I walked out the building's front door and around the corner to the diner. A bunch of booths with red plastic seating faced the windows looking out on Central Avenue. Other assorted tables ringed the enlarged back end of the joint. In front of the grill, a small counter fronted about ten round stools for solo diners like me.

Bud's wife, Betty, worked the cash register. She asked how business was going and gave me a gigantic smile that must have put some pressure on her makeup.

"I just landed a new client. Tell Bud I might be able to pay him rent this month."

Betty laughed. "You know he doesn't care, Arch. He likes having you around. You're like another son to us." I still hadn't gotten used to the friendly nature of the people in Albuquerque after growing up in Phoenix and living most of my adult life in L.A.

I handed Betty a couple of bucks. "I'm in desperate need of a large coffee for the road."

Betty smiled. "Sure, just tell Justine. Where you headed?"

"Up to Santa Fe." I walked to the counter and sat at an open stool.

Justine, a forty-year-old redhead with deliciously abundant hips smiled when she saw me. Her pleasant face benefitted from the little extra weight. She slid a menu across the counter. "Hey, handsome."

"Hey, sweetheart. You look great. Do something different with your hair?"

She ran both hands down her red and white waitress uniform. "Oh, you're such a charmer, Arch."

"When are you going to leave that no-good husband of yours and move in with me?" Her husband was an unemployed carpenter and her salary kept them from starving. We enjoyed playing out our routine banter.

"You just say the word, Arch. I'll leave right now and pack."

"What will Stan say?"

"He won't even notice I'm gone until he gets hungry for dinner. We could be in Miami by then."

"What's in Miami?"

"I don't know. It just sounds good. I'd like to go sit on a beach for a couple of days. I could buy a new bikini and show it off for you."

"You're getting me all hot and bothered, Justine. You better get me a large coffee so I can hit the road before I do something I'll regret. I don't want Stan coming after me with his chisels."

She laughed as she poured the dark liquid into a large styrofoam cup and covered it with a white plastic lid. "Here you go, Hon." Justine referred to all her customers with that moniker, which added to the neighborhood atmosphere, but didn't make the food taste any better. "You have a great day."

I gave Betty a kiss on her rosy cheek and walked out to my car. I checked Frank Minor's list one more time for the Santa Fe address of his ex, Barbara Carson, formerly Minor. I cruised down Central and merged onto I-25, heading north.

CHAPTER 2

The northern sprawl of Albuquerque ends at a series of Indian Pueblos that preserve the colorful mesas and the wide-open vistas of the high desert. Thanks to several thunderstorms during the recent summer monsoon season, the dry grasslands had finally turned a timid green. Despite traveling at 75 mph, the few patches of early fall snow sparkling in the sun on the highest slopes of the Sangre de Cristo Mountains never seemed to get any closer.

The minimal traffic during the 45-minute drive gave me a chance to develop a preliminary profile on Sarah Minor until I turned off the interstate and headed towards the square in the center of Santa Fe. The New Mexico capital city represented an interesting mix of mostly struggling artists and middle-class state employees, along with movie stars and the wealthy who enjoyed living in a slower-paced environment with a hint of culture. The discovery of the city as an alternative to Hollywood caused an inflated housing market, forcing many artists and state employees to go outside city limits to find affordable homes.

The cool September morning air filled the interior as I maneuvered my silver 2006 Dodge Charger up the winding narrow end of Canyon Road to a small, dark adobe building with the address of Barbara Carson's gallery. I squeezed the car into a spot down the street in front of a high-end boutique, and walked back up the hill. The rear of the narrow gallery building seemed to stretch back for a block toward several large cottonwood trees. A low adobe wall shielded a short front porch, and a few paintings and drawings were visible through the glass pane of the front door. A copper plaque said Carson-Kerry Gallery and a cardboard 'Please come in' sign hung in the doorframe, but the round copper doorknob didn't budge.

I stepped around to the wooden entry door on the side of the building, following Frank's directions. Loud classical music reverberated from inside. Rather than knock, I stepped through the unlocked door into a short hallway filled with easels and stacks of unframed paintings. An assortment of smocks and coats hung on hooks to the right of the door. The pungent odor of drying paint and linseed oil filled the air.

I continued down the short hallway and slipped through an archway into a large, dimly lit room. "Hello," I yelled as my eyes adjusted to the gloom. Bathed in soft overhead light, a beautiful young woman with short golden hair stretched out nude on a brown suede divan. Across from her, an older woman, her clothes covered with a blue smock, sat sketching on a stool in front of a large easel.

I averted my eyes from the sprawled goddess and spoke to the artist. "Sorry to intrude, but I'm looking for Barbara Carson."

"How did you get in here?"

"Well, the door wasn't locked."

She addressed the model. "You left the door unlocked." She seemed unwilling to turn her head away from her subject. I shared her reluctance.

"Are you Barbara Carson?"

She returned her attention to me. "That's me. What do you want?"

"I wanted to speak to you about your daughter."

"Look Mr..."

"Call me Arch."

"Arch, I think you should leave." She stood to address me and I saw the refined middle-aged elegance Andy had found attractive.

"It's important we talk."

"I'm busy right now. Can you come back later?"

Barbara glanced to her left and a disturbed look appeared on her face. I caught movement out of the corner of my right eye and turned just as a statue came rushing at my head. My football reflexes kicked in. I raised my right arm to deflect the blow. The statuette bounced off my arm and hit the wood floor with a clatter. I stepped backwards to keep my balance, but stumbled over a large metal toolbox and crashed to the floor among paint-stained drop cloths and wood frames.

From my prone position, the model's smooth muscular thighs and triangle of curly straw-colored pubic hair dominated my view. The mixture of coconut oil and feminine fragrances brought an erotic arousal to my senses. Tension gripped her entire body. A strand of short hair had fallen between her eyes, which were fixed on some distant point.

"I see the carpet matches the curtains." I croaked.

My voice seemed to bring her out of a trance. Her glazed stare reminded me of someone awakening from a deep sleep. Barbara arrived to throw a navy blue robe around the model and usher her through a tie-dyed curtain extending across a doorway at the back of the room. I became conscious again of the loud classical music playing in the gallery, uncertain if the serenade of violins was real or a carnal hallucination.

"You've got a knock-out body," I murmured to the swaying curtain. I pushed myself off the floor and scanned the room. Barbara's half-finished sketch of the nude model rested on the easel. It was good, but no matter how talented Barbara might be, the finished art could not capture the sublime reality of the model's perfection. I heard a door slam behind the curtain.

I rushed after them, pulling the curtain aside. Another hallway led to an exit door at the back of the building. The model's perfume lingered in a small changing room adjacent to the door. A matching set of rose-colored bra and panties, abandoned by their recently departed owner, rested on a small bench. On impulse, I stuffed them in my jacket pocket and exited the back door into a small gravel parking area. A silver Camry, spewing gravel in its wake, sped down the driveway and out onto Canyon Road.

As I walked to my car, the flashing light bar of a Santa Fe police vehicle became visible as it came up the road. I ducked into the boutique and pretended to check a rack of colorful dresses near the window. The cop car stopped in front of Barbara's gallery.

I lost sight of the cops after they left their vehicle and entered the building premises. I slipped out of the store to my car and eased down the road.

In the city's plaza, I found a small restaurant and ordered a cup of coffee. The caffeine alleviated the ringing in my head. During my latter years with the LAPD, I would have already consumed five or six cups by this time of day. To prevent dehydration, I'd kept several bottles of water in my squad car. Chewing gum became another necessity to hide my putrid coffee breath. My addiction had been reduced to one cup in the morning, but half of today's serving sat cold in the container. My harrowing experience in the art studio brought on an acute caffeine craving.

Cops get into some unhealthy habits, with their weird hours and high job stress. I was no different from the rest. I had hit the coffee and cigarettes hard during the day and the booze at night. Joanne didn't need any additional excuses to terminate our six-year marriage. My absences from home left her with most of the responsibility of raising our daughter, who would be turning seven in a week. Joanne had been pregnant with Josie when we got married.

I called Andy Lujan on my cell phone and left him a message. My friend liked playing the field. His Hispanic DNA, which fostered his dark, handsome features, worked like a magnet with women. We became good friends while attending the California Police Academy. Our fellow cadets gritted their jealous teeth when we went out to a local club or restaurant and the women would flock around us. Andy lured them in, but I never complained.

Andy called back after I finished my sandwich. "Well, how is my arch competitor doing?" Andy loved that little play on words. "Did you land a big case or are you desperate to consult with me on my expertise with women?"

"You are so perceptive."

"So, which is it?"

"I'm up in Santa Fe trying to clean up the mess you made."

"Who is she?" With Andy, there was usually a scorned woman.

"Barbara Carson. You know, formerly Mrs. Frank Minor."

"What can I say, Arch? She's a pretty one, but a bit old for me. Ancient news, though."

"Wait until I tell you about this model I ran into. We need to talk. How about I buy you breakfast tomorrow?"

"Sounds good. I just received some information you'll find interesting. What did Barb have to say?"

"Unfortunately, I never really got the chance to talk to her. I think she felt threatened and called the cops." I took a sip of my coffee.

"Don't tell me. You forgot to introduce yourself and gain the client's confidence."

"Yep. I know. I'm not a cop anymore." Andy had repeatedly drilled me on the distinction between being a police officer and a private detective.

"So what happened?"

"I'll tell you tomorrow morning. Barela's at eight?" I decided to cut the conversation short before we fell into our usual pattern of trading cryptic banter.

"Better make it eight-thirty. I've got to meet someone first thing."

"No problem. See you then." I disconnected, finished my coffee, and headed back to Albuquerque. My follow-up questions could wait until I consulted with Andy.

CHAPTER 3

The hot shower relaxed and soothed my neck muscles, still sore from my previous day's tumble in the art studio. During my college football days, even a more vicious tackle would have caused little discomfort.

I anticipated my breakfast would include Andy's friendly ridicule for being blindsided and pinned by a woman. Despite his dismissal from the investigation, I could still sense his continuing involvement. He claimed to have useful information, without specifying whether it pertained to the present case. Andy thrived on the intrigue. His professional life immersed him in a world of movers and shakers, aided by his family's connections to the state Democratic Party. He never hid his political aspirations. To Andy this would be just another case, but to me, a successful outcome would bolster my career.

The parking lot across from Barela's was full, so I drove around the neighborhood before finding a spot. A popular establishment in the historic neighborhood that shared its name, the restaurant provided a meeting spot for power meals and attracted tourists, judges, police captains, and occasionally a mayor or governor. Part of Andy's routine consisted of pointing out various important people. On occasion, I made a valuable connection because, despite being one of his main business competitors, Andy never hesitated to introduce me to someone influential.

Through the glass doors, I encountered a small crowd waiting in the bright blue foyer. The large rooms full of busy chatter made conversation difficult, but the quality of the food made it all worthwhile. My stomach gently rumbled.

The pretty, young Hispanic hostess greeted me with a smile when I asked for a table for two. She nodded and told me to let her know when the other party arrived. I considered getting a table and force Andy to search for me, but he might never make it, being stopped by the many locals who would draw him aside to discuss a piece of local gossip.

As I moved to the rear of the entrance hallway, I had a flashback of the long, slim thighs of the model from the gallery. She had fixed me with a sad, almost apologetic stare before disappearing as if she felt remorse for nearly cracking my skull. My infatuation with her reminded me of my lack of female companionship since my split from Joanne. Despite my faults, Joanne said she would always love me, but living with me was like a long-term internship in purgatory.

The "internship" comment referenced her extended sentence while serving at the county medical examiner's office when we first met. She had worked 60 hours a week for little pay, no benefits, and the pleasure of getting the nastiest assignments. She must have seen the similarities in our marriage; only our union offered little hope of a future reward.

My cell phone read 8:45. The usually punctual Andy was late. But he had mentioned meeting with someone first thing that morning. I peeked through the double glass doors, expecting to see Andy striding toward me, but there was only a cluster of young professionals in their business suits and red power ties gathering on the sidewalk.

As the group entered the restaurant, I glanced to see it was almost 9:00. I called Andy's cell phone, but got no answer. What the hell was keeping him? I waited another fifteen minutes and then drove over to his modest house near the University where he'd let me stay when I first moved to the Duke City, the natives' name for this high desert metropolis. Andy loved the house and never considered moving unless he got married, which seemed unlikely given his playboy persona. Besides, I suspected he considered the location optimal for picking up college girls.

Andy's black SUV sat in his driveway as I turned onto his street. I pulled in behind it, expecting him to come loping down the porch steps spouting apologies. I knocked on the door several times and rang the doorbell, one of those yellowed plastic strips, but I couldn't hear it ring. I moved to my right and peered at the shadowy living room through the slit in the dark curtains. There appeared to be a light on in the kitchen at the back, but I couldn't detect any movement.

Not getting any response, I decided to check for the key hidden under a large gray flowerpot on the side of the house. Self-conscious about being observed, I walked confidently, taking a glimpse around before lifting the pot to remove the key. A car alarm sounded down the street, piercing the quiet neighborhood, devoid of faculty and students on a fall weekday morning.

I opened the front door and waited for the alarm to sound, but noticed it had not been set. I called out Andy's name and loudly identified myself several times. Andy packed a mean Smith and Weston .45 and I didn't need him confusing me for a burglar. My yells were greeted by dead silence.

The house had that unsettled smell of a single male, something I recognized in my own place. The living room contained sparse furniture—a small brown leather couch and two matching chairs, a flat screen TV and stereo system, and a large wine rack along the left wall. Andy loved his red wines and the bottles filled every available space.

The room's wood floors continued down a hallway to the kitchen and the sound of my shoes cut through the stillness. In the kitchen, I turned off a dripping sink faucet. The pair of small bedrooms and his quaint office at the rear of the kitchen were empty.

I crossed the kitchen to the foyer where a sliding glass door exited into the backyard. Andy's body stretched facedown and half way out the open door. A blood trail led down the back of his polo shirt and onto the floor.

"Shit, Andy." With the amount of blood, the odds were against his still being alive. I checked in vain for a pulse and collapsed against a massive chest freezer.

Suddenly conscious of not being armed, I searched for a weapon and grabbed a titanium club out of the red golf bag leaning against the corner of the hallway. Gripping the club, I checked the house, but the drying blood on the floor confirmed the shooting had occurred much earlier and it was doubtful the murderer had stuck around for a meet and greet. Streaks of blood extended across the corner of the kitchen wall at the entrance to the back room.

I needed to call the cops, but I also wanted some time to figure out what had happened to Andy before the APD chased me out. Andy's smart phone lay in the yard leaning against a struggling patch of grass just beyond his outstretched hand. Tears welled up in my eyes as I slipped out to my car to retrieve a small notebook and a pair of nitrile gloves for handling the phone.

I turned the phone on expecting a request for a password, but after sliding the indicator to unlock, the screen lit up with a series of applications. A couple of taps brought me to the list of recent calls and I got busy copying the numerous numbers and names. I returned the phone to its place in the grass, tucked the gloves and notebook into my jacket pocket, and called 911 from my phone.

A duo of uniformed cops showed up minutes later followed by a Detective Burns from the Criminal Investigation Department. I knew Burns, thanks to an introduction from Andy about a year ago. He ambled in the front door, wearing a navy blue jacket to cover a white shirt protruding at various points from his overweight belly.

Despite his rumpled appearance, Burns was a sharp detective who had been fond of Andy. Having a military background, Burns still sported his blond crew cut to remind us all of his service. A small piece of tissue paper clung to his neck where he had cut himself shaving. Being divorced, he no longer had a partner to check his appearance before he exited the front door. With a deep frown plastered to his grizzled veteran face, he walked straight to me.

"Hey Burns." I didn't know what else to say. He shook my hand, the gloves and notebook a guilty lump in my breast pocket. Eventually, I would have to come clean about handling the evidence.

"Arch, what the hell? Someone shot Andy?" Burns eyes shifted around the kitchen. One of the uniformed cops nodded to him as he noted the location of a shell casing.

I shrugged. A bullet doesn't distinguish between a good man and a creep. Too bad I hadn't arrived earlier with my gun for a chance to plug a few in the degenerate murderer.

One of the first officers to arrive had taken my statement as they locked down the scene, awaiting the arrival of the detectives and CSI. Burns waited for me to repeat my statement to him. He pounded on a pack of cigarettes, pulled one out, and stuck it unlit between his lips. He didn't offer me one.

"I was supposed to meet him at Barela's this morning at eight-thirty. I tried calling him, but didn't get an answer. I finally drove over and arrived just before nine-thirty. I knew he kept a spare key under the planter outside so I let myself in. The front door was locked."

"No sign of forced entry." Burns nodded.

"Doesn't look like it. They must have slipped out through the back yard."

"And he was half outside like that?" Burns was a chain-smoker and even in the morning, his fetid nicotine and coffee breath burned my nostrils. His suit had absorbed the daily cigarette smoke, and the stale odor combined with the aftershave he used to hide it was lethal. I tried not to breathe too deeply, remembering my own struggles to shake those same habits.

"Yeah, it looks like he got shot from behind while in the kitchen, went down and pulled himself up along this wall." I pointed to the white plastered corner with the bloodstains sliding at an angle. "Maybe he fell again and dragged himself to the door trying to make a call before he died."

"He was shot at close range." Burns walked gently to the rear door, avoiding Andy's prone body.

"No doubt, maybe by someone he trusted enough to let into his house." I stayed put and glanced the other way.

"Damn, he was a good man, Arch."

"He told me he had an early appointment and couldn't meet until eight-thirty."

Burns turned back to me. "He didn't say with whom?"

"No, unfortunately."

"Any idea what case he was working?"

"No, you know Andy. We didn't discuss our cases with one another unless we were working together." Which wasn't exactly true. The discussion usually consisted of me consulting Andy on one of my cases, including my current one. I wasn't quite ready to tell that to Burns.

"Yeah, I figured. I'll need you to come down to the station with me so we can get your official statement. Did you touch anything?" He glanced around at the crime scene.

"I was careful, but my prints are probably on this chair and the freezer in there." I pointed to the backroom containing Andy's prone body. "I checked Andy's neck for a pulse and I picked up that golf club as a weapon just in case. That should be it."

"Okay. You carrying?"

"No, it's why I grabbed the club, but I guess you've got to check." I raised my arms to make it easy, acknowledging that my presence at the crime scene made me the initial suspect.

"Yeah, I forgot you know the drill." He patted me down and I flinched as he brushed the pocket with the notebook and gloves.

Burns led me to the door. "I'm sorry, Arch. I know he was your friend."

"Thanks Burns. I know you're just doing your job."

He took me to the station where I gave another statement and then sat in a crowded holding room for an hour before Burns came to retrieve me. "Your record is clean. I sent a plainclothes over to Barela's with your photo. Seems your story checked out. You must have made a real impression on the hostess; she remembered you right away. You're free to go."

"Can I call Andy's family?"

"Just give me until later today."

I nodded and shook his hand again. He walked me through a maze of corridors to the front lobby desk where an officer returned my phone and wallet. Burns assigned a young uniformed male cop the task of driving me back to my car at Andy's house.

After arriving home, I pulled out the notebook and began copying the names and numbers to another sheet of paper. Burns wouldn't be happy with me for handling the phone, but asking for forgiveness seemed easier than requesting permission that would have been denied. He seemed like an honest cop, but my experience with the LAPD taught me it was hard to know whom to trust—even locked evidence occasionally went missing. After completing the list of numbers, my hunger cravings returned as a reminder of my cancelled breakfast.

CHAPTER 4

"What the hell?" Burns shot forward almost falling out of his chair after I walked into his office and dropped the list containing Andy's call history. "I needed the names of his contacts and recent calls. I plan to find out who murdered him."

Burns shook his head. "I should book you for tampering with evidence from the scene of a crime and obstructing a murder investigation, you asshole."

"Before you blow your top, I made a list of all the names and numbers, so I saved you the work. There's a bunch of entries represented only by numbers you could check out. I figured he communicated recently with whoever shot him."

"That was a bonehead move, Caldwell. We've already got someone working on it."

"Look Burns, I'm an honest Joe. You can ask Sergeant Anaya or Officer Keane. They know me pretty well. I used gloves and handled the phone carefully. And I didn't delete anything." I could see my coddling wasn't placating him at all so I figured I had to give him something. "I was hired by this guy named Frank Minor to find his daughter. Frank told me Andy had an affair with his ex-wife Barbara, an artist in Santa Fe. Her number is on the list. I didn't have any luck speaking with the ex, so I figured the best thing would be to talk to Andy first. That's why we were meeting for breakfast." Frank's number appeared on the list, and despite being my client, he was going to have to fend for himself. I wouldn't be much help to him in jail.

Burns seemed to calm down a bit. "Was Andy still seeing this ex, Barbara?"

"No, I got the impression he had broken it off." I sat down on one of the chairs across from Burns' desk.

"We could have a jilted lover. What about the ex-husband? Revenge?"

"I doubt it. They've been separated for a couple of years and divorced six months ago. I got the impression there was some cooperation to find the daughter."

"Don't fuck with me Caldwell. I'm going to let you slide on this, but if you pull something like this again, I won't hesitate to throw your ass in jail. Am I clear?" Burns leaned back and gave me a smug smile.

"Perfectly. Andy was my friend. I want to know who killed him. We have a mutual interest. Frank had originally hired Andy to find his daughter, but it seems Frank may have lost confidence in him after the affair and hired me. About all I can tell you at this point. I just got started on the case."

"So, we can assume his death may have something to do with this case you're working on?"

"Like I said, I haven't had a chance to do much investigating. But, Andy told me on the phone he had some information for me that might be useful."

"About this case?"

"I can only assume, since he never got a chance to elaborate."

"Alright, Caldwell. I expect you to keep me informed about anything that even smells like this investigation."

I had given him the Andy-Barbara-Frank connection so I figured I could ask at least one question. "What about the ballistics?"

Burns eyed me and his voice hinted at what could only be described as admiration for my boldness to ask. "Shot at close range in the back, probably with a silencer. None of the neighbors we talked with heard anything. Time of death somewhere around eight o'clock. We'll know more after the analysis."

I nodded and pushed myself up from the chair. "Thanks. I'll let you know what I come up with. Here's my card."

He tossed it onto a disorganized pile spread across his desk.

"Just don't fuck with me, Caldwell." He repeated it as if for shock value, or perhaps he wanted to sound military tough. He didn't scare me and his threat wouldn't keep me from pursuing Andy's assassin.

"I got it, Burns. I'll stay in touch." Andy would have figured out a way to smooth things over with Burns. I struggled to find a peace offering, but nothing came to mind.

"You're lucky you're not a suspect. You handled evidence at the scene. You should know better. If I thought you were the killer, you'd be sweating in interrogation."

"I understand." I got to his office door and stopped. "Let me know when I can call Andy's family. I'm not looking forward to it, but the news might be easier coming from a friend."

"Sure, you can save us the effort. The news will hit the papers tomorrow morning. APD will need to notify them as per protocol."

"Thanks Burns." I liked Andy's family and almost regretted my offer. I exited the office before Burns could blast me again.

Upon arriving home, I went directly to my "medicine" cabinet below the TV in my small living room for the bottle of Jack Daniels. I poured a good shot and dumped it down my throat. The bottle accompanied me into the kitchen where I fixed a tall "jack and coke" before returning to the living room. Quitting cigarettes had been difficult, culling my coffee consumption had been rough, but my battle with the bottle would be postponed. I thought about my wife and Josie with a sigh. Who needs love when you've got Jack Daniels?

I needed a good buzz from liquid courage before I could call Andy's family. Even though I had performed this formal rite of death several times with the LAPD, I never got used to breaking the bad news to the victim's loved ones. My toughest moment had been informing a Korean mother of her teenage son's killing in an apparent neighborhood gang related drive-by shooting. The woman's anguished cries ripped at my heart as I left her to grieve, hoping she had someone else in her life. Later, I tried to drink myself into oblivion to erase the memory of the woman's despondent wails in a language I couldn't understand.

I always feared becoming indifferent to or losing my angst over a death. Like the war movie about soldiers whose job it was to notify the families of loved ones killed in action. A few soldiers got used to it as a routine and required psychological counseling to live normally and be able to experience grief. Enough stalling. Calmed by another slug of Jack Daniels, I reached for my phone.

"Hello, Mr. Lujan. This is Arch Caldwell." My voice cracked.

"Hi Arch. How are you?"

"Mr. Lujan. I have some very distressing news." My eyes filled with tears.

"Andy?"

I took a deep breath. "He was shot and killed this morning in his house. I'm so very sorry."

A prolonged silence followed before he asked what happened. I gave him a summary of the few details available. He thanked me for calling instead of leaving it to the police. He hung up to call the remaining family members.

I mixed another drink and called for a pizza delivery—a night of drunkenness had arrived with little chance of my interrupting it to go out.

The stress of announcing the death of a loved one reminded me of my own estranged family. My relationships with my father and brother were nearly dead—the relationship with my mother on life support. Feelings for my daughter still burned as her birthday approached, but I had never exercised my visitation rights. I considered following up with my contact to get an updated address for my ex-wife, but hated the thought of dealing with anyone back in L.A. Besides, the less the LAPD knew about my whereabouts, the better. Andy would have called in a favor and had the information discreetly provided with no questions asked. My friend and that option were no longer available.

I knew Sergeant Robert Anaya at APD could get me an address. I had been friends with Robert since high school, but asking him to track down my ex-wife made me a bit uncomfortable. I didn't want to put him in the awkward position of having to refuse. But he owed my family, or should I say, my father. Robert had never applied himself academically, and his application to the Arizona Police Academy had been rejected. Thanks to my father's influence, Robert's application received a second review and subsequent acceptance. After four years with Phoenix Police, he moved to Albuquerque for a job with the APD. He continued to communicate with my father, who no longer spoke to me. It didn't matter. After sharing the sorrow with Andy's father, it became essential not to let my daughter slip out of my life. I took a deep breath and an even deeper gulp of my drink before dialing Robert's number.

CHAPTER 5

I drove back to Barbara Carson's studio the next day hoping the model would be present. The image of her beautiful body remained vivid in my memory.

The gallery lights were on as I opened the front door to a tinkling chime from the Nutcracker Suite. Barbara looked up as she sat at a small metal desk engaged in a conversation with a woman whose back was to me. Her eyes followed me around the gallery as I pretended to be interested in the artwork until my attention was drawn to a group of pencil sketches of nude women. I searched for a rendition of my attractive attacker. Unfortunately, the drawings were abstract, featuring the partial torsos of models, with little detail to make a positive identification.

Wandering around gave me an opportunity to observe Barb. I could see what had attracted Andy to this woman. She resembled a slightly aged Angelina Jolie, with dark hair and eyes, and full lips. I figured her for mid 40s. As she stood to say goodbye to her guest, her shapely curves became evident.

Easing back into her chair, Barbara glanced at me. "I'm glad you came back."

"You are?" I looked around in an exaggerated manner. "Where's the cavalry today?"

"I'm sorry. Jesse gets a little protective sometimes. We didn't know who you were. And you were asking about my daughter. I called Frank later and he confirmed he had hired you."

"Jesse." The name didn't fit the vision. I took a stab. "There's a facial resemblance between you."

"Jessica, she's my oldest daughter. She got the blond hair and height genes from Frank."

I struggled to digest this news flash while maintaining my poker face, making a mental note to talk with Frank about not revealing Sarah had a sibling.

"And I'm sorry for her violent reaction. She suffers from cataplexy, it's a form of narcolepsy."

"You mean the sleeping disorder?"

"Yes, sort of. She used to have attacks accompanied by paralysis and hallucinations. As she got older those episodes were reduced to what the doctors called automatic responses to fear, where she acts out certain behaviors without being fully conscious of what she's doing."

"That makes sense. As she left yesterday, she had a glassy-eyed stare as if she had just woken up from a dream."

"It's pretty common. The episodes used to include lots of screaming and cussing, but that's improved. I hope she didn't hurt you."

"No, luckily I reacted in time to avoid being hit with the clay statue. Hopefully, it wasn't one of your prize works."

"It was just a project I started and never finished. One of many. It's the life of an artist." I could tell she was warming up to me, at least a little. I motioned to the lone chair and she nodded for me to sit. "Can you help find my daughter?"

"Yes. May I call you Barb?"

"Of course. If you're going to be intimately involved with the case, we should be on a first name basis."

I flashed her with my best smile. "In case Frank didn't tell you, my name is Arch Caldwell, Call me Arch."

"Yes, he told me."

I sat back and let my smile fade. "Andy Lujan is dead."

She showed little emotion at first, but gradually her shoulders slumped as her hands went to her face. "Oh my. How?"

"He was shot yesterday. The cops interviewed me for several hours since I was the one who found the body. They'll want to talk to you."

Her hands dropped to her lap and she looked at me. "We stopped seeing each other about three months ago. It was a mutual decision."

"Do you know if Andy was still working on the case?"

"I'm not sure. After we split, Frank called to tell me he planned to hire another private detective. I spoke with Andy only once after our breakup. He was still pursuing some leads. I told him Frank was going to hire someone else, but obviously I didn't have your name."

"I was supposed to meet him yesterday and discuss the case. Unfortunately, someone killed him before we met." Andy would have known Frank had hired me. Only a handful of private detectives operated in Albuquerque. Unfortunately, the number had been reduced by one, a fact that brought me no consolation. "When was the last time you saw Sarah?"

"Six months ago. She stopped by the studio. She was living with her father and said they had had some kind of argument. I told her she could stay with me. She looked strung out, tired. I was worried about her and tried to get her to tell me what was going on. She told me to mind my own business and left. Jesse may know more."

"Are they close, Jesse and Sarah?"

"They are now. Sarah is younger and more rebellious, despite getting everything she ever wanted. When Jesse was younger, she resented Sarah for all the attention we gave her, but as Jesse matured, she began to take a greater interest in her sister. Their friendship developed as Sarah pulled away from Frank and me."

"Do you know where I can find Jesse?" I hoped not to sound like an infatuated teenager.

"She'll be here again in about a half-hour. As you already discovered, I've been using her as one of my models."

"So I gathered. I'd say it was a good choice, with all due respect. The good looks certainly seem to run through the female side of the family. Frank gave me this picture of Sarah." I placed the photo on the desk. "Do you have any more recent photos?"

"That was taken at dinner on her sixteenth birthday. She's seventeen now. It's the most recent photo we have, but I have other digital pictures if you need them."

"This should be fine. You said she looked strung out. Do you mean high or drunk?"

Barb hesitated. "She has a drug problem. Frank thought it was just pot, but Jesse and I suspected she was doing something stronger before she disappeared. Frank was always a bit naïve about drugs. She wouldn't talk to any of us about it. Jesse and I encouraged Frank to hire Andy because we didn't want the cops to find her first, if you know what I mean."

"I understand. What have the cops told you?"

"Very little. We filed a missing persons report with the Santa Fe police, who issued an amber alert. They don't seem to be doing much."

"Okay, I'll check with them to see if they've gotten any response. I'll also need to talk to Jesse. Hopefully, she no longer feels the need to plant a sculpture in my skull."

Barb smiled. "I told her about you. You'll get a warmer reception."

"I hope so." I reached into my wallet. "Here's my card. Call me if you think of anything else that might help me locate Sarah."

"Can you find her?" Barb's voice quivered, tears formed at the corner of her eyes and threatened her attempt to be stoic.

"I'll do everything I can."

She tentatively accepted the card. "I'm real sorry about Andy. We had fun while it lasted."

"Andy was a friend of mine and I'm going to find his killer." I stood up. "Is there any reason Frank would still be jealous of Andy?"

Barb gave me a half-hearted smile. "Frank hasn't been jealous in many years, and besides, he's got himself a young girlfriend. He's certainly not capable of killing anyone. Nor am I."

"I didn't think so, but my instincts tell me Andy's death is related to this case. Please call me if you think of anything. I don't want to disturb your time with your daughter so I'll catch Jesse later."

I returned to my car down the street from the studio. After several attempts, I connected with Detective Cordova, a friend of Andy's with the Santa Fe police. Cordova had heard the news about Andy and agreed to help me. There had been several tips reported, none of which resulted in a positive identification of Sarah. He promised to keep me updated on any new potential leads.

Fifteen minutes later, Jesse walked up the sloped street carrying a large handbag. Even at a rapid gait, her hips swayed effortlessly, not exaggerated like a model strutting on the runway. She wore a drab maroon uniform with white tennis shoes. The garb didn't diminish her beauty. Just the sight of her got my heart pounding, a feeling lost since my early days of courting Joanne. To my disappointment, she rounded the corner of the studio building.

I didn't want to miss Jesse when she left the studio, so rather than search for a cup of coffee, I pulled out my notebook. Andy knew Frank had hired another detective and my call must have confirmed it. That's why Andy was amenable to meeting me for breakfast the next day. Normally, when we discussed getting together for lunch, he put me off for days and sometimes weeks. But this time he seemed anxious to share information despite the romantic split with Barb and getting fired from the case.

And there was the cell phone. I was convinced he intended to call me with the murderer's name before he collapsed. A dying man doesn't worry about apologizing for being late for breakfast. What he had learned about Sarah's disappearance must have gotten him killed.

I waited in my car with the windows open as the cool morning departed, replaced by the promise of a warm fall afternoon. Visitors paraded up and down the road, stopping in various galleries. I assumed Barb informed Jesse about my return visit. After twenty minutes, a group of three women entered the front door to Barb's gallery. Jesse appeared around the building corner a few minutes later.

As she started down the hill, I exited the car and stood by a black metallic fence running parallel to the sidewalk in front of another gallery. As she approached, a wave of recognition rolled across her face. She made no effort to avoid me, which was a good sign.

"I figured you were still hanging around." She didn't bother to stop. I launched off the fence and struggled to keep pace with her long strides aided by the downhill slope.

"Can I buy you a coffee or something else to drink?" I abandoned any hope of sounding professional.

"Sure, there's a nice tapas joint on the next block. We can sit outside."

"I'm sure your mom told you, but my name is Arch Caldwell."

She stopped for a moment and I stumbled to slow down my momentum. "Yes. I'm Jessica. But my friends call me Jesse."

"Can I call you Jesse?"

"I don't know. Are you my friend?"

"Not yet. But I'd like to be."

She smiled. "That was a pretty honest answer, although a tad corny." She continued walking toward the restaurant.

"Well, I may be corny, but I would never use a colloquial word like 'tad'."

She laughed as we stopped on the sidewalk in front of the cement wall shielding a long patio with Parisian style tables. The sign read "El Farol." She climbed the short staircase and turned toward me at the top. "Come on, let's have some lunch."

"Sounds good."

We sat on stools at one of the roundtop tables and, despite the comfortable temperature, we were the only patrons sitting outside. A waiter emerged from the interior of the restaurant. We ordered iced teas and accepted lunch menus, which featured an assortment of interesting small-plate servings.

"I'm sorry about the other day. Apparently, I didn't hurt you."

"You felt threatened by me." I posed it as a statement knowing about her medical condition.

She looked away toward the street. "Yes, I guess so."

"Who did you think I was?" She squinted at me furtively. A long silence followed, as she appeared to be deciding her next step. I waited, nervous as a junkie anticipating a fix.

"I'm not sure. I was responding to your inquiry about Sarah and reacted badly. We're all very upset by her disappearance."

"Of course."

"I have a condition and I don't always maintain control."

I took a deep drink of my iced tea. "Your mother told me about it. A form of narcolepsy."

She hesitated. "Cataplexy. I went through years of behavioral therapy and the doctors gave me all kinds of medication. I'm not against all drugs. As a nurse I know the right prescription can occasionally help people with serious illness. But some drugs have side effects worse than the disease."

"What did they do to you?"

"They brought on more irrationality and paranoia. I stopped taking all except the one prescription that works for me. If I don't remember to take it, I can have a relapse like yesterday. I'm sorry."

"No need to apologize again. It's just something to be aware of since we're going to become such good friends."

"That's awfully presumptuous, but I like your spirit. She smiled. "Are you hungry?" The server had arrived with our drinks and now stood anticipating our order.

"Just a tad."

Her laugh sounded more like a stifled giggle, but was endearing. "How about splitting some tapas with me? I have to go to work in a few minutes." She studied the menu and then me. "What do you like?"

"Whatever. I'm not too picky. Have you eaten here before?"

"Yes, a couple of times. Everything's good."

"Then I'll defer to you and assume as a nurse you'll select something relatively healthy." My outstretched right hand pointed to the menu as an invitation. "Order away."

She smiled. "I don't always practice what I preach. How about roasted potatoes, cheese polenta, and maybe the salmon to be on the healthy side? You look like you need some Omega-three."

"How could you tell? Those are the three dishes I would have chosen."

She confirmed our order with the waiter and took a sip of her drink. "Mom said I hit you with a statue. It's pretty embarrassing."

"It was a small one. Luckily, you were in a half-catatonic state otherwise you might have done some damage. You seem to be very athletic."

"I played volleyball. I was on the Olympic team briefly." She shrugged as if it was no big deal.

"Like your father."

"Yes, we have that in common." She smiled. Her short strawberry-blond hair and bright eyes reminded me of the actress, Jennifer Aniston. Jesse's toned athletic structure complimented her tall frame, and her face glowed of self-confidence, despite having a severe medical condition as a constant companion in her life.

Knowing I could get lost in that vision, I peeked out onto the narrow street and directed the conversation back to business. "When was the last time you saw your sister?"

"Back in April. At Casa Esensio in Albuquerque. I went down there with a guy I was dating. You know the place?"

"Yeah, not that I hang out there. A bit too upscale for me. Was she alone?"

34

"She was with this Freddie somebody, who looked like a pimp. He surrounded himself with tough guys who acted like former cops." Her eyes pierced into me.

"We're that obvious, are we?"

"I've dated one or two." She said it so casually, I couldn't be sure if being a former cop might be appealing or repelling to her.

"So, you thought I might be one of this Freddie's henchmen."

"I wasn't sure. It seems silly, but I don't always think rationally." She fixed me with an apologetic grin.

"Your father thought I could help locate Sarah. I guess he didn't feel like he could trust Andy Lujan anymore."

"Ah, yes. Andy Lujan. My mom told me."

"I know he dated your mother."

"He hit on me, too."

"Sounds like Andy." I smiled reluctantly. What would he have made of my interest in Jesse? He'd no doubt encourage me to pursue her.

"He was a friend of yours." She said it as a statement of fact. She probably figured us male law enforcement types were always conspiring against members of the opposite sex.

"Yes, we knew each other for years. Despite what you might think of him, he was a great guy." I tried to keep any hint of sorrow from my voice, but the sadness must have flashed briefly across my face.

"I'm really sorry." A frown appeared on her face and she reached across to touch my hand.

"Thanks. You're very insightful."

"It comes with the territory. Nursing isn't much different from being an investigator. Patients don't always want to tell the truth about what is ailing them and without that information it is more difficult to treat them effectively. So sometimes we have to piece together the medical mystery."

"If I were your patient, I would probably spill my guts. I mean that figuratively, of course." The first serving arrived, which saved Jesse from having to respond, and me from further embarrassment. I asked about her relationship with her father.

"We have a professional relationship."

"What do you mean?"

"He talks to me like I'm one of his clients, instead of his daughter. Since I'm four years older, he expects me to act differently than

Sarah, so he communicates with me more formally. He doesn't do it intentionally."

"It's funny, but he never even mentioned he had another daughter."

"Sounds like my father, the lawyer. He gives you just the 'need-to-know'. But when I make him feel guilty about something, he usually capitulates and tells me the full details. Something to remember when you want more information....or money from him."

We made small talk for a while. After we finished the last plate of marinated salmon, I returned to business. "Can you tell me more about Freddie?"

"He was flashy."

"In what way?"

"You know, the one hundred dollar haircut and a baggy, chartreuse colored pimp suit. A size too big."

"Can you give me a more detailed description?"

"Dark. Tall. Hispanic. Handsome if you like the type." I tried to read whether or not that applied to her, but she gave no indication.

"How was your sister that night?"

"She was high on something. Her eyes were red and pupils dilated. Not normal. I have enough experience to recognize the symptoms."

"You think it was drugs and/or alcohol?"

"She was drinking, but her physical appearance and anxiety made me suspect cocaine. I tried to talk to her, but it was so loud and Freddie kept close tabs on her. I wanted to take her away, but she didn't seem willing to leave."

I nodded. "Around those people, cocaine would likely be readily available."

We chatted a while longer before she glanced at her watch. "I've got to run or I'll be late. I'm due at the hospital for the afternoon shift in about fifteen minutes." She said it ruefully, not dismissively, as if she actually enjoyed my company. I thought it was a good omen.

"Well that explains the outfit." Now the purpose for the lackluster clothing became clear—to mask her sexuality and prevent a heart patient's demise from cardiac arrest after seeing her sashay into the hospital room.

"What did you think, I worked at Burger King?"

"No, nurse would have been my first guess." I lied. "How about I drive you over?" I left thirty dollars with the bill under one of the glasses and we walked to my car.

Before starting the car, I reached into the back seat and handed her a small paper bag containing her bra and panties. "This is embarrassing, but I thought I might need these for a DNA test."

She peeked inside. "I wondered what happened to these."

"Sorry. I'm not a pervert or anything."

"We'll see. Thanks for returning them." She smiled and stuffed the bag into her purse as I pulled out onto Canyon Road.

Unfortunately, in a small city like Santa Fe, nothing is very far away. We arrived at the Christus St. Vincent Regional Medical Center too soon. She asked about my police career, but I barely had time to begin the saga before we pulled up in front of the Surgical Services Building. She opened the door to get out.

"Jesse. I may not be the greatest detective in the world, but I'm persistent enough to find your sister."

She turned to me. "I'm sure you will. I'm just afraid of what you might discover. Thanks for lunch and the lift."

She shut the car door, but I couldn't bear to just let her walk off. "I may have more questions. Where can I reach you?"

She leaned in through the window. Like fairy dust, her faint musky perfume drifted over me. "Jessica Minor. You're a detective. I'm sure you can figure out how to get in touch with me." Her sarcasm hung in the air as she walked into the hospital. I wanted to kick myself for being such an idiot.

• • •

I called Frank, chewing him out for not telling me about his older daughter.

I heard Frank groan. "Oh no. Sorry. So you met Jesse?"

"Why didn't you tell me about her?"

"I was going to. It's a bit embarrassing, so we don't speak about it much. She has a type of narcolepsy."

"I know."

"She's had it since childhood. We didn't know what it was at first. She didn't even speak much as a child. One day, Barbara had her in a shopping cart at the grocery store and some woman bumped into the cart. Suddenly Jesse told the woman to fuck off and nailed her in the head with a box of cereal."

"Perhaps the woman deserved it." Frank ignored my crude attempt at humor. Of course, the situation probably wasn't funny from the father's perspective.

"She will lash out both physically and verbally when she feels threatened. She takes medication, which seems to moderate the effects."

"Okay, I'll let it slide. Any other vital information you want to tell me?"

"No, I'm sorry. I didn't think you would run into her this quickly."

"Can you tell me about some of Sarah's friends? I'll need to talk to them."

"Her closest friend is Pamela Simmons. Her info is on the contact sheet I gave you. You might catch her at Santa Fe High School. Sarah didn't have a lot of friends, at least those we knew of."

"It will be a good place to start." I disconnected and pulled out Frank's summary wondering what other important details he might have excluded. Andy had probably already talked to Pamela, but his death forced me to re-trace his now cold footprints.

CHAPTER 6

After several wrong turns, I located Santa Fe High School, perched on a hill and protected by a tall black iron security fence. A young guard, decked out in his navy blue uniform, greeted me at a small wood shack protecting the school entrance. He advised me to check in at the student services desk and directed me into a parking lot.

Leaving the parking lot, I passed below a cement façade noting that the school was founded in 1899. The new brick and mortar exterior suggested that the school had received a recent facelift. Several more guards mingled outside with the students, enjoying the mild fall weather.

The receptionist on the second floor of the administrative building stared at me suspiciously as I approached the oval Formica fortress surrounding her. "Yes sir. How can I help you?"

"I'm here to see a student." I fumbled for my credentials and handed them over. "I'm investigating the disappearance of one of her friends."

"You'll need to meet with the principal. Just a moment." She picked up the phone and punched in a four-digit number. After a short conversation she turned back to me.

"Someone will be down to escort you to the Principal's office."

I thanked her and waited five minutes before a young female student with pink braces, a nose ring, a double-pierced ear, ripped jeans, and a long blonde ponytail, arrived to escort me down the hall to the Principal's office. She frowned and stared down at the floor the entire trip past multiple offices.

We stopped outside a recessed doorway. A pudgy middle-aged man with dark thinning hair wearing a bland gray business suit emerged from the open door to greet me. The girl disappeared as I shook the hand of Principal Griffith. He gestured for me to sit across from him after we retreated to his office and he settled behind his desk.

"What can I do for you, Mr. Caldwell?"

"I'm investigating the disappearance of Sarah Minor. I was hired by her father." I handed him my private detective certificate.

He scanned it and handed it back. "Ah, yes. Sarah. I'm certainly aware of the case. Her parents have been worried sick. I hope you find her. How can I help?"

"She has a friend named Pamela Simmons. I was hoping to ask her a few questions."

He seemed to think about that for a moment. "I'll need to verify you're working for the Minors."

"Of course. Here's Frank's card with his cell phone number."

Principal Griffith accepted the card. "Thanks, but I'll use the contact information in my computer." He tapped the keyboard before dialing a number. A short conversation with an intermediary ensued until Frank got to the phone. "Mr. Minor, this is Principal Griffith. I have a…" He glanced at my card. "Arch Caldwell here who says he's investigating Sarah's disappearance."

The principal listened, nodding with the conversation. "Thank you, Mr. Minor. Of course, we will help in any way we can to find Sarah."

He hung up and smiled. "I'm also required to obtain permission from Pamela's parents." He consulted his computer screen again and dialed a number without success. He re-checked the screen and dialed again. This time he connected, and after consulting with someone, appeared to get the necessary permission. He hung up and nodded to me. "I'll have someone retrieve Pamela from class. It will be a few minutes. You'll have to conduct the interview here in my presence."

I nodded and relaxed as he made another call to someone responsible for tracking down Pamela Simmons. Based on the information provided by the family, she appeared to be one of

Sarah's few friends. It was surprising such a pretty senior didn't have numerous girlfriends, or at least attract more attention from the boys.

My thoughts had turned to my daughter, Josie, and what she might be like in high school, when a tall thin girl came to the door. Beneath her long, coal black hair she wore a short brown leather skirt and green sweater. Principal Griffith rose from his chair and invited her in. "Mr. Caldwell. This is Pamela Simmons."

I shook her hand, offered her my chair, sliding over to its companion.

Principal Griffith pre-empted my introduction. "Mr. Caldwell was hired by Sarah Minor's parents to find her. He wants to ask you a few questions."

She nodded and peered straight at me.

"I'm sorry to have to pull you from your class, but this won't take long."

She shrugged. "It's no problem. Another guy like you came to my house and asked about Sarah."

"Do you remember his name?"

"No, but he was a detective like you."

"There was another private detective working on the case. Are you good friends with Sarah?"

She nodded, but added. "We are, but I haven't seen her in a while."

"When was the last time you saw her?"

"It's been like since the spring sometime."

"Was that the last time you talked to her?"

"Well, she texted me."

"When was that?"

"I'm not sure. Maybe April."

"Do you still have the text?"

She shifted in her seat. "No, I checked when the other detective asked the same question."

"Do you remember what she said in the text?"

"She was going to live with her father and maybe get a job for the summer."

"Anything else?"

"She said something about hangin' out at a club in Albuquerque."

"Did she mention any names?"

"No, it was just a short text."

"Is there anyone else she hung out with in Santa Fe?"

She glanced at Principal Griffith.

"It's okay Pam. Mr. Caldwell is trying to find Sarah so any information you provide will be helpful."

She spoke softly. "There's Troy."

"Who's Troy?"

"I don't know his last name. He's older. Sarah dated him briefly last year. Her parents didn't know about him."

"How long did they date?"

"Maybe six months."

"Can you tell me anything about him?

"He has long hair. He looks kind of like a hippie."

"How can I find Troy?"

"He attends Santa Fe Community College. And he has a really cool car."

"Can you describe it?"

"An old bright red sports car. Like a Mustang, I think."

"Well, it should help find him. Anything else she might have said that could help us locate her?"

She shook her head. "I can't think of anything. I'm sorry."

"It's okay. You've been very helpful. Principal Griffith has my phone number, so if you do think of anything else, please let him know." I thanked her as she left the office. The principal accepted my card, wished me luck, and promised to contact me with any new information.

I checked my Santa Fe city map in my New Mexico Gazetteer, but it didn't include the community college. I pulled into a gas station near the interstate and got directions. I followed a road called Dinosaur Trail, imagining a line of prehistoric animals falling into tar pits to be preserved for the rapture of future paleontologists.

I turned south on Richards Avenue and drove through an undulating landscape of parched grasslands mixed with juniper trees. The rural area seemed an unlikely location for a community college until I ascended a slight rise and noticed the symmetry of brand new residential developments erupting on both sides of the road. Many homes stood in various stages of construction among recently paved driveways. The fresh growth of the community around the college explained why it didn't show up on my outdated map.

The college appeared on my left and I suddenly found myself in a bizarre traffic circle preventing a turn into the parking lot. Finally, after going around a second time, I found the correct lane and entered the college.

The campus consisted of limited parking areas, which made my job of finding a red Mustang easier. Driving around the main lot, I spotted the shiny, sultry vehicle parked among the traditional metallic blue, silver, and green cars. It looked like an expensive antique car. Too expensive for a kid going to a community college. I could barely afford the maintenance on my Dodge Charger.

I parked across from the Mustang and waited, leaning against my car to soak up the remaining warmth as the sun descended in the western sky. The wind, a reliable New Mexico tradition in itself, chilled the mild autumn temperature.

A Grateful Dead sticker was plastered like a scar on the bumper of the Mustang. Why would someone want to blemish a vintage sports car? The remainder of the vehicle's exterior didn't have a single imperfection. The interior hadn't held up quite so well. The front leather passenger seats were littered with wrappers, books, pens, and empty Starbucks coffee cups. The trail of debris extended into the car's rear bucket seats, cluttered with songbooks for The Beatles, Led Zeppelin, and the Doors. Evidently, Troy's taste in music favored classic rock. I guessed he played an instrument.

I returned to my car. An hour later, students began trickling out of the buildings. A guy with long reddish-blonde hair headed towards me.

As he got closer, I noticed a goatee, dark blue jeans with bleach spots, green Converse sneakers, and a checkered dress shirt loosely tucked into his pants. He could have been a handsome guy if he lost the 60's flashback look.

"Nice car." I said as he stepped up to the Mustang.

He turned as if just noticing me. "Thanks. It's a sixty-seven. I did a lot of the work to restore it."

I exaggerated my nod and gave him a pinched grin to let him know how impressed I was with his work. "Are you Troy?"

"I might be. Who's asking?"

"Arch Caldwell. Pamela Simmons gave me a description of your classic car and said I might find you here." I reached out my hand and he shook it with a firm grip.

"What can I help you with, dude?" He looked suspicious as if trying to determine whether I represented the Man.

"I'm a private detective, not a cop. I was hired by Sarah Minor's parents. She's disappeared and they're quite concerned. I was hoping you could help me."

He frowned. "Yeah, man. I'm bummed she's gone. I really dug her."

"Do you know where she is?"

"No, man. I'd tell you if I did. She was a great chick, but got too much into the drug scene. I mean we smoked some grass, but you know, recreationally."

I shrugged, not sure what he defined as recreational pot smoking. "When was the last time you saw her?"

"Wow, maybe four months ago. She tried to get me to come down to Albuquerque again and I said no way."

"What do you mean 'again'?"

"She was hanging out with these well-dressed dudes who had a lot of money and drugs, going to fancy clubs and shit. It wasn't my scene, man. I want to get an education, do something meaningful with my life. I thought she felt the same way, but when she started hanging out with that crowd, I knew we were through."

"Do you remember where you went or anything about the people she was hanging out with?"

"We went to a couple of fancy clubs on Central, you know, downtown. I can't remember any of the names. I was pretty fucked up that night because I knew we were breaking up. I don't remember anybody's names either. It was the last time I saw her."

"Have you communicated with her since then?"

"Yes, we were texting each other about three months ago. Then we broke up. I was pretty bummed, but didn't know what to do, you know? I mean she wanted things I just couldn't afford for her, man."

I shook my head to let him know I got it, although I was dubious that a high school romance required such a high level of commitment.

"Tell me about those other people Sarah was with in Albuquerque?"

"I don't know. There was this one Hispanic dude hitting on her and trying to ditch me. Like I said, it's a bit fuzzy. He reminded me of a pimp because of all the hot women surrounding him. I'm sorry, man, I can't remember any more details."

I reached into my wallet and handed him my card. "Thanks Troy. Please call me if you remember anything else."

"Yeah, sure man. I hope you find her and she's all right. I didn't trust the dude she was with."

"You're the second person who said that. You play an instrument?"

"Yeah, guitar. How'd you know?"

"Chord books in your back seat. I'm a detective."

"Yeah, cool. Well, I gotta cruise. Band practice tonight."

I shook his hand again. "Thanks for your help. Good luck in school and take good care of that car."

"Oh yeah. You know it, dude." He turned, using his hand to pull back his straggling hair from his face. Once in the car, he turned on the ignition, the engine roared to life like an adult male lion and then settled into a quiet even cub-like purr as he backed out. He nodded as he drove past.

I made it about halfway back to my car before he stopped and slowly backed the car up. As the rumble of his car settled, he addressed me through the open window with an apologetic wave. "I just remembered. Sarah had another friend she hung out with who may know more about those guys down in Albuquerque. I don't remember her name, but she worked at a Mexican restaurant called Manny's Café near the Santa Fe plaza. I saw her there not long ago, so she probably still works there. Sorry, it just registered, man."

"No problem. What does she look like?"

"She's pretty, but goes for the punk rock thing. You know, short spiked hair and lots of piercings."

"What color is her hair?"

"Dark. She's a bit on the heavy side."

"How old?"

"Not sure. About my age. Early twenties."

"Thanks, I get the picture."

"No problem, dude." I guess he had forgotten my name already even though I had just handed him the card. Maybe he had watched the *Big Lebowski* too many times.

Troy drove out of the parking lot. Without a smartphone, I had to find the restaurant the old-fashioned way by paying extra to call 'Information.' If this new case brought in enough dough, I could afford to buy a new phone.

• • •

Manny's Café resembled a small adobe fortress on Palace Avenue just down the street from the plaza in the center of old town Santa Fe. I envisioned a Mexican drug cartel snuggled in with their weapons behind the tall tan blockade. The wall next to the restaurant entrance featured a painting of a typical desert southwest scene, complete with dramatic mesas sliced by plunging canyons in front of an ancient adobe church. Above the church, a cloudless sky formed a solid blue horizon, as though the artist had run out of white paint.

I entered through the screen door into a bright room with a small bar to the left. The reception podium was vacant, but behind the bar, a tall bartender in a white apron covering a blue dress shirt nodded to me as he stood drying glassware. "You need a table?"

"Yeah, one for dinner."

"Inside or out?"

"Seems like it's going to be a nice evening. I'll sit outside."

"We've got a nice patio if you keep going down the hallway. It's pretty slow this early, so just go out and sit. Tanya will find you."

"Thanks." Another screened door appeared at the end of the hallway. Green wood tables and matching chairs huddled behind the tall curved adobe wall. A barrier of juniper poles stood wired together, the end posts bolted to the adobe wall and attached to the large wood beams that stabilized the roof. Uneven rows of juniper poles rested on the pine beams running across the under surface of the roof. The intertwined Christmas lights must have become a permanent fixture.

An older couple sat at the only other occupied table, nursing a couple of margaritas. They ignored my arrival. I decided not to spoil their experience and chose to sit at a small table on the opposite side of the patio. My table and chair wobbled slightly on the uneven flagstone floor. Hummingbird feeders and clumps of bright red chiles hung from the ceiling like grapes on the vine.

A waitress appeared and checked on the elderly couple. They had hardly touched their drinks, so with a smile she headed over to my table.

Her short black hair lay unevenly on her scalp like a lava field. Her ears, nose, right eyelid, lip, and, as I realized when she spoke, her tongue were all pierced with some type of small shiny ornamental globes. She could have been pretty, if she ditched the purple lipstick and the S & M theme. She stopped in front of my table and pulled out a small notebook. "What can I get you?"

"Well, I was going to order a margarita, but that couple doesn't seem to be enjoying theirs very much."

She laughed. "They come in for happy hour every now and then, order margaritas, eat the chips and salsa and then leave. I don't think they're big drinkers, but they order a drink so they can munch on the chips."

"Sounds like a pretty good plan. I'll try one. Without salt." She nodded and headed off to the bar.

She handed me a menu when she returned with the drink, and a basket of chips with a cup of salsa nestled inside. "Just in case you get hungry, the food's pretty good here. The green chile chicken stew is my favorite."

I ordered a bowl. A deep sip of margarita brought immediate refreshment. Before the waitress brought the food I had finished the drink and ordered another. She returned and hovered by the table. "What's your name?"

"Arch. Are you Tanya?"

"Yeah, how'd you know?"

"Bartender mentioned your name."

She moved in a bit closer. "So, Arch. What brings you to Manny's?"

"A kid named Troy over at the community college said this place had good food. You know him?"

"Yeah, I know Troy. How do you know him?"

"I don't really. I got his name from Pamela Simmons. He gave me your name. I'm looking for Sarah Minor. Her father hired me. He thinks she might be in trouble. I was hoping you could help me find her."

She gave me a stern gaze. "Let's see some ID."

I pulled out my private investigator certificate and my driver's license and handed them over to her. She scrutinized them for about twenty seconds before handing them back. "You look better in person."

"Thanks. Sarah's family is very concerned about her. There hasn't been any contact with her in at least four months."

"Well, I'm not sure what I can tell you. I haven't heard from her in a while."

"When did you last talk to her?"

"She called. I'm not sure how long ago."

"Can you give me an estimate?"

"Probably about the same time. Four months ago."

"Can you remember anything about what she said?" I took a sip of my drink.

"She hooked up with some slick Hispanic guy in Albuquerque. The guy liked to spend money on her. She bragged about some expensive necklace he bought her." Her smile gave me the impression she was sizing me up to determine if I might be in a similarly lucrative position.

"This Hispanic gentleman have a name?"

"Freddie. Freddie Martinez. I'm not sure why I remember his last name."

"You're the first person I've spoken to who could. Did she tell you anything else about him?

"No, she seemed really into this guy. He had money."

"How did she sound?"

"Sarah's emotionally elusive. She bragged about snorting coke with the well-to-do, but she didn't sound very happy."

"What made you think she wasn't happy?"

With a scrape of the chairs on the flagstone, the older couple headed for the exit. Tanya glanced over at the vacant table and then at the couple's retreating backs. "Have a nice evening." On the table, a mound of singles and the bill lay fluttering in the breeze. She turned back to me. "I don't know. Just the tone of her voice. Like being stuck in a situation with no exit if you know what I mean. Though she seemed to be enjoying having some money thrown at her."

"Well, they say money doesn't buy happiness."

"It's a convenient saying, Arch Caldwell. I'd like to test it out sometime."

She used my full name with a hint of intimacy. Would she have slept with me if I could also lavish her with pricey gifts? Well, I doubt I could have gotten past the spiked hair and all the facial jewelry. "So, you think she had become hooked on drugs?"

She shifted her weight and put her hands on her hips. "Duh, yeah. Why do you think she was there?"

If Sarah had become an addict, it would make my job of bringing her back much more difficult. "Thanks. That's helpful." I reached into my jacket. "Here's my card. Please call if you think of anything else."

"No problem. Are you staying in Santa Fe tonight?" She flashed me a seductive smile with her pierced tongue, effectively turning me off.

"No, I have to get back to Albuquerque."

"Too bad. You're kinda cute."

"Yeah, but I'm not rich."

"I wasn't lookin' to get married."

I laughed, being too old to blush. "It's a good thing, you're too young. I tried it once."

"What happened?"

"I screwed things up. I've got a daughter." I'm not sure why I added the last part, except maybe to emphasize the differences in our age and let her down easy.

She seemed to get the hint. "If you find Freddie and he isn't treating Sarah right, you kick his ass for me. Okay?" She turned and strolled back into the restaurant, not bothering to wait for a reply.

Tanya came back out with the bowl of stew and the check. I finished the stew and downed the remainder of the drink. I dropped two twenties for an $18.50 bill. The tip was mostly for the information, but maybe I appreciated her hitting on me. It was the thought that counted. I slipped back out through the restaurant to my car.

CHAPTER 7

Detective Burns called me with a partial confirmation of the ballistic info. Three bullets had entered Andy's body at close range. No one heard the shots. The killer used a silencer. Before he died, Andy had dragged himself to the sliding glass door that opened to his backyard. The police found Andy's blood on the lock and handle, evidence of his Herculean effort to reach the yard in his last moments of life. He must have known I would be the first one to reach him after he failed to show up for breakfast. Perhaps, he had gripped his cell phone in one last struggle to call me. Or maybe his effort to reach the yard represented a message to me. That possibility had me awake and slipping out of my apartment at 2:00 am.

I cut the headlights and eased past Andy's house. The yellow police investigation tape formed a netted barrier across the front porch. I drove around the corner and parked, returning to the house to retrieve the hidden front door key, the police failed to remove. I cut through the cat's cradle of yellow tape and opened the front door, severing the multiple taped seals. I hoped the neighbors were sleeping soundly. I didn't want to further test Detective Burns' patience with me.

I turned on my flashlight, equipped with a glued-on shield made out of a white plastic University of New Mexico Lobos cup with the bottom cut out. The cup surrounded the round glass face to focus the beam of light and reduce the possibility of someone on a late night stroll seeing the reflection. I also put on a fresh pair of nitrile gloves, part of my ample supply provided by my ex-wife from the

L.A. Medical Examiner's Office. Given the paucity of cases in my new career, the box could last a lifetime.

In Andy's office, I dug through the papers in his desk to locate anything related to his murder. I turned on his computer, which oddly hadn't been removed by the police. The computer prompted me for a password. I tried dozens of combinations, including the names of his father and mother, but nothing worked. Then it hit me. He and his sister Beverly were extremely close and his nickname for her was "babushka." I tried it with no luck, then added a "1" and the computer delivered me to a blue screen highlighted with a rainbow of program links and documents.

I searched his folders until finding one labeled "Sarah Minor." The contents represented insignificant case notes and scanned copies of invoices paid by Frank Minor, confirming Andy had been well paid for his services. I spent a few more minutes going through the hard drive just to make sure I hadn't overlooked other secret folders with cryptic names. Disappointed, but not surprised, I turned off the computer. Andy was unlikely to leave important information regarding his cases vulnerable on his computer. The police had probably already checked and reached the same conclusion.

There had to be something else. I recalled Andy mentioning the intel he wanted to share. It became clear Andy had to be referring to something beyond this current case. He died trying to reach the yard. The backyard.

I stumbled when the subdued beam of my flashlight illuminated Andy's partially chalked outline sprawled across the backroom floor. The drawing included just the bottom of the torso as if the top had been severed by the door. I had witnessed cops killed in the line of duty, and gazed over a few chalk figures sketched on a floor, but none that belonged to a close friend. With a deep breath, I recovered my composure, knowing Andy would have ridiculed any feelings of grief. He would have encouraged me to "get on with it" and find the evidence left for me. If I had been the murder victim, Andy would have pursued the culprit with a dogged persistence.

I stood there, inside the sacred perimeter of police evidence tape. Andy's enigmatic presence guided me through the back door. I eased the glass and screen doors aside, stepped into the moonless yard to feel the night breeze caress my cheek. Despite the crickets chirping, the cool fall night was tranquil. I searched the yard, crouching below the six-foot concrete block walls, and directed the flashlight toward bare patches of dirt, checking for recent soil disturbance. The yard contained no gas grill, lawn chairs, nor garden. A silver metal shed stood in the corner of the small yard.

I opened the unlocked shed door, curious to see what Andy had stored. A few rakes, a hoe, and one of those short shovels a height challenged person might use leaned against the shed wall near the entrance. The garden tools presented a mystery, given Andy's complete disdain for yard work.

The shed had plenty of space as I stooped to enter the five-foot doorway entrance. A strong smell of desert earth tickled my sinuses. The wind picked up, and the draft through the shed's permeable corners made a slight whistling sound. I stepped back to the doorway and stuck my head out to listen. The breeze gained momentum and kicked the leaves of a neighbor's tree in motion. A plastic bottle clicked, skidding across a hard surface somewhere nearby. The shed door started protesting against the wind and clanked against the side wall of the shed. The noise seemed excessive to me, but probably not to the neighbors. I stepped back out and wedged the door open with the rake. A siren sounded from a police vehicle speeding several blocks over on Central Avenue. As the siren faded, I stepped back into the shed.

A thick black tarp covered the metal shed floor. As the flashlight flittered around inside, my gaze returned to the tarp. Why a tarp on the floor? I shined the flashlight along the edge of the shed wall where it met the floor and startled several gigantic crickets. I reached down and pulled unsuccessfully at the tarp, tucked into the crevice between the shed wall and the floor. I picked up the shovel and gently tapped on the floor. The soft clink of metal on metal persisted until I reached the center where the shovel dug into a soft surface below the tarp. Further probing revealed a missing square foot piece of the floor. I returned to the edge of the shed, but could find no break in the cloth tarp.

A pile of gray concrete blocks, commonly used to create a perimeter yard barrier, reflected off the beam of my flashlight. The blocks were stacked neatly against the back wall and resembled a low pyramid conforming to the shape of the shed. The blocks seemed out of place for a man who never met a domestic project he liked. Andy thought the cable station HGTV provided 24-hour coverage of the human genome project.

I removed the blocks, placing them on the side closest to the door. Underneath the blocks, the tarp was loose and I pulled it past the missing square piece of the shed floor. In the flashlight's halo, the soil appeared to be recently disturbed. I dug using the mini-shovel, carefully piling the soil on the backside of the tarp next to the hole. I connected with something metallic after excavating a foot of soil. A few sweeps with my hand uncovered the top of a cashier's lock box, the size of a phonebook, which I removed after scouring out the surrounding soil. The temptation to open the box was overpowering, but another distant siren persuaded me to urgently fill in the hole. My intuition told me the box contained whatever Andy had wanted to share, but opening it would have to wait.

I pulled the tarp back across the floor, replaced the concrete blocks to their original position, and slipped out of the shed. I dusted off the remaining soil from the box and dropped the flashlight into my jacket pocket. I removed my soil-covered shoes, carrying them with the box while securing the interior of the house. I peeked through the drapes in the front window to make sure my path out would go undetected. Once on the front porch, I reached into my jacket pocket for my roll of police evidence tape to replace the original strands as closely as possible. I put my shoes on, returned to the car, and with nervous hands placed the lock box on the passenger seat.

CHAPTER 8

I delayed opening the box after arriving home. I crammed my soiled clothes into the washer, cleaned my shoes thoroughly, and took a shower, scrubbing away my criminal excursion—entering and then removing a piece of evidence from the murder scene.

Pouring myself a strong shot of Jack Daniels with Coke as a garnish, I studied the box on the coffee table before trying to pull up on the metal latch to release the lid. The latch didn't move. There was a slit for the small narrow key not in my possession.

I found my Leatherman tool while fumbling around in the kitchen drawers searching for a strong narrow knife. The Leatherman's small knives and a narrow file proved too large to function as a substitute key. I retrieved a small crow bar from my gray plastic toolbox. Placing the box on the floor and kneeling on it with all my weight, I wedged the crowbar in the space between the latch and the lid. The latch bent with the pressure and the lock catch released with a pop.

Several white business envelopes sat atop three large manila ones folded to fit in the cramped interior. The first small envelope contained only sheets of paper with dates, dollar amounts, and series of numbers. It took me a minute to realize the lines represented deposits made to a California bank in Pasadena. The remaining business envelopes had similar information from other banks.

The first manila envelope contained a thick set of white paper sheets bound with a tight rubber band. The first few sheets appeared to be transcripts from an interview or maybe a deposition—the participants referenced by initials. A nervous sweat formed on my forehead as I realized the two-letter monograms belonged to my previous fellow officers in the LAPD. Digging further into the document, I saw the initials AC, and recognized my own words muttered to the Internal Affairs agents a year ago in an interrogation room at LAPD headquarters. I experienced a flashback of my four hours of quasi-accurate testimony poisoned with half-truths.

I spread the contents of the second manila envelope across my coffee table. Several photographs featured my ex-partner, Benny, meeting with other force members and people indicted in the scandal. Rumors circulated during the hearings that case evidence had disappeared, helping secure our acquittals. Some evidence had found its way to Andy's ownership. Why, and more importantly, when did he get this information? On the phone, he hadn't been referring to the Sarah Minor case after all. I had to suspect this information, now in my hands, could have led to his murder.

The significance of the contents made my head spin. My eyes could no longer focus on the print. The remaining manila envelope would be opened later after I had a good rest. I leaned my head back on the couch cushions after sucking down a healthy portion of my drink. Unlike my father and brother, Andy had always believed in my complete innocence. His faith in me was mostly warranted. The vanished evidence and my incomplete testimony resulted in the subsequent case dismissal and acquittal of the accused. Did Andy suspect I might have been complicit in the failure of Internal Affairs to prosecute those rogue cops due to my inconsistent testimony? Andy knew the ropes better than anyone. He would have recognized my vague responses as self-preservation. Perhaps he had planned to present this evidence to me and encourage me to pursue my own justice. Now, I would never know.

My troubled mind swirled, re-living that fearful chaotic time in my life, and it kept me awake despite my exhaustion. Andy's support and advice had been a big part of my defense. Could he have actually been more deeply involved? The possibility haunted me until I finally fell into a stupor just as the light of day made its unwelcome appearance.

CHAPTER 9

I slept until the middle of the afternoon the next day, showered and collected the various documents bequeathed to me by Andy's unfortunate death. I needed to get these envelopes safely out of my apartment.

My first stop was the Duke City Bank, one of the few remaining family-owned financial institutions in the city. They didn't offer much service, but my minimal financial cache required few member perks. They did have safe deposit boxes to store my documents including a note of instructions on their disposition if I followed Andy to the grave. The FBI would salivate over this evidence, but for the present, it would stay protected until I could further evaluate my options. If Andy's death was related to the documents, then my life would now be in danger if someone found out they were in my possession. Andy had been investigating the Sarah Minor case, but I couldn't establish a connection between her case and the incriminating evidence in the box. I ruled out the Minor case as a reason for his murder, turning my attention to tracking down this notorious Freddie Martinez.

I stopped by the office to retrieve my K-frame Smith & Wesson Model 19 .357 Magnum, inherited from my dad and used throughout my career, despite the many newer models available, like the standard 9mm issued by the LAPD. Andy's murder convinced me to start carrying a weapon. Like Andy, I was more than proficient with a gun. We used to finish together at the top in marksmanship back at the Academy, cultivating a friendly competition that cemented our friendship. But having a gun and being skillful with its use didn't help much if you got bushwacked from behind. I looped the Sam Browne belt around my pants, slid on the Don Hume Tiger Revolving Holster, and slipped the gun neatly into its place before heading home.

I taped the safe deposit box key to the back of the icemaker in my freezer at home, a safer place than my office. Dinner consisted of leftover pasta from a white styrofoam box, heated in the microwave. I couldn't remember how long the food had been in the refrigerator, but it tasted fine.

Dressed up in a nice pair of khaki slacks and a navy blue sport coat, I drove down Rio Grande Boulevard arriving at the Hotel Albuquerque parking lot just after 9:00 pm. I hid the gun in the car and made the short walk over to Casa Esencia, the hot late-night joint located in a renovated 8,000 square foot hacienda on the outskirts of Old Town. I didn't visit the club often, but had recently attended an APD retirement party there, thanks to an invite from Andy.

The place didn't open until 10:00 p.m., but my early arrival didn't ensure a prompt entrance. It always helps to know someone. After dropping a name and paying the twenty dollar cover charge, I was admitted through the sacred doorway into a dimly-lit open-air courtyard. A lighted, shallow, rectangular reflecting pool in the center of the open space added to the club's elegant décor.

I walked past a well-dressed bartender, returned the smile of a pretty young woman in a revealing turquoise dress, and continued my rounds. My brown leather loafers clunked on the rich teak colored hardwood floors. I arrived at the Piano Room, a large candle-lit space with cream-colored couches and chairs, and gold lampshades. A black grand piano defined the far end of the room.

The man I had come to see stood against a wall in an interior corridor talking to a group of ladies. He smiled when I approached. "Arch, you must be desperate for lovin' to come to this place." I shook the hand of Roger Cornelius, the joint's security chief and another acquaintance courtesy of Andy.

"Ladies, say hello to my friend, Arch Caldwell."

Several of the women smiled and said hello reluctantly, acting as if I had intruded on their party. Roger dominated the conversation with his rich Southern drawl. Besides being tall, dark-skinned, and handsome, Roger could charm the pants off most women or men. I suspected he might go either way given the right opportunity. A former marine, Roger still sported his close-cropped curly service hairdo. He looked thin in his black suit, but exuded a military strength he could employ if things got rough with the late-night revelers. He dismissed his groupies and we walked down one of the corridors into another bright room with elongated white tables and art nouveaux high-backed chairs.

"You got a serious frown like you investigatin' something."

I turned to Roger. "I'm actually looking for a guy. But not in the sexual way."

Roger laughed. "Good thing. I thought maybe you'd switched to the other side of the plate."

"No, I probably couldn't hit from that side either. Football was my sport."

"Yeah, right. You a UCLA dude. If I were a few years older, we may have faced one another. Did you guys ever play Fresno State?"

"I don't recall, but then I got hit so many times, my memory escapes me."

"Nothin' wrong with your memory, Arch. Tight end?"

"Too small. Wide receiver. Defensive end, right?"

"You got it. Played three years and not a scratch. Second week in Iraq and I got a load of shrapnel in my leg. It's why I limp some."

"Never noticed."

"VA do a good job, but sometimes on a cold day, whew, I can still feel them lead fragments, like they was still there."

A couple of early arriving attractive co-eds walked by and greeted Roger with a seductive hello. Two things got you into the club early: knowing someone or being dressed like you stepped out of a Victoria's Secret catalogue.

He turned and gave me a conspiratorial shrug. "Who you lookin' for?"

"A pretty boy named Freddie Martinez. Heard he hangs out here."

"Yeah, I know him. I haven't seen him yet, but he'll likely be here tonight with some doll on his arm. What's your business with him?"

"Not sure exactly. I'm hoping he'll help me find a young lady who went missing. Andy was working the case until he was killed."

Roger's jaw dropped. "What you sayin', Arch? Andy's dead?"

"Yeah. Sorry Rog, I figured you knew. Shot in his house. It's been all over the local news."

"Damn, Arch. I don't watch the news. What are the cops sayin'?"

"They don't have much. I'm not sure if his death is related to the case I'm working. If so, it might involve this Freddie character."

"Let me know what I can do. Andy was a cool dude." He shook his head.

"Yeah, and a good friend. I intend to find out who killed him."

"Damn straight. Why don't you have a drink and relax?" He death-gripped my elbow and lead me to a concave aluminum art deco bar in the corner of the room. "Hey, Conrad, give this man a drink on me." He turned back to face me. "I'll let you know when he comes in. But you take your business outside."

I nodded and he headed back to conduct his rounds or maybe track down some luscious co-eds. Conrad waited as I considered a drink of something fruity mixed with alcohol, settling on a peach mojito. Not my usual taste, especially given the hefty price tag. Maybe the classy atmosphere confused my taste buds. If you wanted to see the rare decadent upscale side of Albuquerque, this was the place. The beauty of the mostly younger women reminded me of Jesse. What would she have said if I'd invited her?

I strolled around the bar checking the rooms—a ritual usually reserved for newbies to the scene. Each of the dozen open rooms featured a completely different style. I chose a comfortable leather couch, the color of crème brulee, in a dim room that opened to a larger bright one where a sizeable crowd gathered. I sipped my tangy drink, occasionally catching a glimpse of Roger as he drifted through the raucous hordes.

An hour later, Roger appeared at the room entrance and made eye contact. I followed him down a corridor to a large, bright, crowded room where he nodded as he stood behind a tall Hispanic man with a pretty blonde who had her arms looped through his in a stranglehold.

I could see why the women were attracted to this guy—his strong dark features created an aura of mystery, and he had just the right amount of chin stubble to give the false impression he didn't give a damn about fashion, despite arriving in a perfectly pressed one thousand dollar suit with the big-breasted female as his cuff link. His perfectly trimmed straight hair didn't have a single strand out of place, unlike the curly chest hair protruding from a grayish-blue silk shirt open at the collar to reveal a gold cross trying not to get buried.

I killed another hour pretending to have a good time, but kept a close watch on Freddie. Out of respect for Roger, there would be no confrontation inside. However, if he knew this Freddie had any information on who plugged Andy, he'd be the first one to initiate an interrogation and he wouldn't have needed waterboarding to get a confession.

A third mojito swirled in my stomach by the time Freddie appeared to be making motions to leave. After a diet of white wines and snuggling, his blonde companion must have been lubed in all the right places. She hung on to Freddie's arm like a lifejacket as her right foot tipped, threatening to bust out of her high-heeled shoe. Freddie might have a sure thing even without the booze.

I returned to the parking lot, stopping at my car to retrieve the gun from the glove compartment. My position at the parking lot perimeter provided a direct view of the club exit. Freddie and his date emerged a half-hour later. I started walking slowly towards the rear of the parking lot when it became evident his car sat behind the building. The shadows would work to my advantage. I also counted on his being distracted with thoughts of getting his date home.

Freddie stopped at a black Porsche and let his companion in the passenger door. His car selection made me dislike him even more. I removed my keys and hovered next to an adjacent white SUV pretending to search for the appropriate key.

The trunk end of his car backed up to some dense shrubs against the building, forcing him to walk around the front of the vehicle. I launched, and grabbed him around the throat, pushing his body into the shadows up against the short trunk of his fancy car.

"What the fuck?" He started to reach down to his leg, but I pinned him down and pulled out my gun to dissuade him from going for a weapon.

"Don't do anything stupid." I warned, pressing him more firmly against the car.

"Look, I got some money in my wallet." He frantically searched the parking lot as if to call for help, so I placed my gun to his forehead.

"I don't want your money, Freddie. I just have a few questions and if you tell me the truth you can be on your way to enjoy the rest of your evening."

That seemed to settle him down. "Okay, man. What do you want?"

"I'm looking for a young girl. You know her. You with me?"

He nodded to let me know he understood. His companion rolled down the window. "Freddie, what's going on? I'm not feeling too good."

I motioned with my gun and shook my head sideways. "She does anything stupid, I'll have to club your pretty face."

Freddie nodded. "We'll leave in a minute, babe. Stay in the car."

"I think I'm going to be sick." Her blonde head slipped down below the seat backs.

"You're going to have a fun ride home, Freddie. Just tell me about the girl and you can go." I released my pressure on his chest, but kept the gun out just in case.

He started to smooth down his clothes. "I know a lot of young girls."

"I'll bet you do. This one is special. Her name is Sarah Minor."

"Who?"

I gave him a short left jab to his jaw. "Don't piss me off. Not only is that her last name, but she was under-aged when you were doing her. You tell me where she is and that information doesn't need to go any further. You read me?"

He put up his hands. "Okay. I haven't seen her in months."

I could tell he was reluctant to tell me something so I brought the gun back up to his head. "You're really making me angry."

He cringed. "She became a fucking mess. She was beautiful, but her appetite for drugs was non-stop. I couldn't afford to have her hanging around anymore."

"Sure, Freddie. You couldn't afford the drugs. What happened to her?"

"I don't know. I dumped her."

"When was this?"

"About five months ago. I told her I didn't want to see her any more, but she kept coming back here. She wouldn't leave me alone. I had the bouncers keep her out of the club because she'd make a scene." He hesitated again and I pressed the gun to his head.

"She was seventeen years old, Freddie. What did you expect?"

He raised his hands. "Man, I had no idea. She said she was twenty-one. She looked older. Really, I had no idea."

"I don't care. I just want to find her. Tell me what I want to know and I'll leave you alone." A few people had filtered out into the parking lot and I lowered the gun against my jacket where Freddie could still see it. The small group walked by, glanced at us, and quickly looked away. It was status quo these days. Just mind your own business and stay safe.

"So, what happened to her?"

"I called a guy who specializes in girls."

"You mean prostitutes?"

"Yeah, he took her off my hands by promising her lots of drugs."

"You're a real bastard. Who is he?"

"They call him Coney. Short for Marconi. That's all I know."

"How did you get in touch with him?"

"By phone."

"You got a number?"

He nodded. "I need to get my phone." I backed up, but held my gun where it posed an immediate threat. He raised his hands, and with his right extracted an iPhone from his suit pocket. He read off the number while I entered it into my cell phone with my left thumb.

"You better hope she hasn't come to any harm or I'll be back to find you. And I won't be this gentle." I didn't consider myself a tough guy, but the urge to unload on that miserable creep was overwhelming. I kept my gun on him and back-stepped away from his car, glancing around the parking lot. Freddie got in his car and I retreated to mine across the lot. Freddie pulled out onto Rio Grande with a screech of tires followed by a tracer of smoke.

I crossed another parking lot into the Hotel Albuquerque and greeted the female receptionist at the front desk. "My cell phone died. Can I use your phone to make a quick local call?"

I dialed the number Freddie had given me and hung up when a man with a New York accent answered. "Yo, this is Joey."

I shrugged at the receptionist. "It was the wrong number. Thanks." The phone rang at the receptionist desk as I slipped through the doors.

Back at home, I checked Marconi's number against the list from Andy's cell phone. Sure enough, the number matched several calls Andy had dialed or received two days before his death. The case had gotten more interesting.

CHAPTER 10

My call to Jesse provided an excuse to hear her voice, but the request for assistance was valid. "I need your help."

"For what?"

"There's a guy who was involved with your sister's disappearance. I'll need a woman with your credentials to draw him out."

"I take it you're not referring to my nursing experience."

"No, but someone might need first-aid."

"You?"

"I'm hoping it's the other guy."

"What did you have in mind?"

"I need you to help me get him alone so I can extract the necessary information."

"So, I'm the bait."

"Yes, but I'm reluctant to ask because it could be dangerous."

"Will it help find my sister?"

"I think so."

"I'll do it."

"How's tomorrow night? I'll pick you up so you don't need to risk driving."

"It's no problem. I'll take my medication so I don't whack the bastard before you can find out where Sarah is located." Jesse's voice crackled in my ear. I didn't argue.

. . .

Freddie Martinez lived in a wealthy neighborhood in northeast Albuquerque. His street ran uphill through the neighborhood of high-priced homes surrounded by empty spaces filled with large boulders and prickly-pear cactus.

I checked the address provided to me by Officer Cordova of the Santa Fe police, and edged past his house, a red brick mansion with white trim. A double-wide white chained gate protected the driveway that led to the three-car garage on the uphill side of the house.

The brightness from the setting autumn sun reflected in my rearview mirror as I parked and waited down the street. As darkness descended, a coyote emerged from the empty lot in front of my car, crossed the road, and entered the backyard of a neighboring house.

At about 8:00 pm, Freddie's Porsche eased out of the garage and down the driveway. I slumped down in my seat as he exited the car to open the gate. I heard him pull through and stop. I got out of my car and crossed the street as he closed the gate behind him.

He turned and saw me leaning against his car. "What the…not you again?"

"Running solo tonight, huh Freddie?"

"What do you want from me now?"

"I want out of your life, but I need one more thing first."

"What?"

"Marconi might be calling you to ask about me. If you rat me out, you better hope he gets to me before I get to you."

"Yeah, but he might just take me out first."

"I doubt it. You're just directing some business his way. You don't know anything about me, except what I tell you: I'm a married man looking to unload my girlfriend. You stick with the plan and everyone will be fine."

"Except Marconi."

"I've got no intention of hurting the man. I just want to find the girl and bring her home."

"And then you'll leave me alone."

"You got it."

Freddie drove off in a hurry and I returned to my car. Using a disposable cell phone with an unpublished number, I called Marconi, fabricating a story about having a wife and a drugged up girlfriend. The wife was getting wise and now I needed to unload the girl. Marconi sounded suspicious, until I mentioned Freddie's name.

Marconi wanted to meet me at a club called Low Spirits down on 4th Street. I knew the place, although I hadn't been inside. It had a reputation as being a biker bar, but with progressive rock music. He told me to dope the girl and bring her and five grand. I had Jesse, but not the money. That made me nervous.

CHAPTER 11

Jesse walked into my office wearing a short silky red dress with a plunging neckline. I had told her to wear something partially revealing, but wasn't quite prepared for such a heavenly sight. "Wow." I muttered before recovering enough to apply some fake hair onto my upper lip.

She laughed. "Is that your full disguise?"

"No, I have another piece." I donned a pair of clear glasses and stood to show her my gray conservative business suit and red tie. I wanted to resemble an accountant coming straight from the office. "What do you think?"

"You look just like a rotten cheating husband."

"Exactly what I was going for."

"Did you learn Disguise 101 at private detective school?"

"What private detective school? I've got a PE degree from UCLA."

Jesse grinned. "Well, that explains everything."

It was a five-minute drive from the office to the bar in my rented Chrysler LeBaron, a car I assumed a two-bit philandering accountant might own. I gave Jesse a summary of my new plan and she agreed to everything. I didn't lie to her about the dangerous people we might encounter.

"It's worth any risk to find my sister." I would have adored her for her spirit alone, even if she had been ugly and wearing a potato sack.

Parking spots were plentiful around the bar's neighborhood and parking lot, indicating a light happy-hour crowd. I parked in the back by a large dumpster. We sat for a moment, waiting for darkness. The lights around the parking lot flickered on, bathing the car in a dim light. It provided enough visibility to see Jesse's body as she lay in the rear on her side, facing the back seats to reduce the chance of Marconi identifying her later.

I got out and leaned through the open back window. "Are you ready?"

"Sure." She sat up and reached out to adjust my moustache. "Your disguise is falling apart." Her touch was warm and comforting; her hands didn't tremble like mine. She must have had more confidence in me than I did.

I walked around the opposite side of the building and entered the bar. Small groups formed around a series of high-top tables in the center of the elongated room. The clientele consisted of an interesting mix of college kids, business people, and bikers. I ordered a Jack and Coke and inquired about Marconi. The bartender nodded toward the opening in the rear room containing several billiards tables. I dropped a ten dollar bill on the bar counter next to my untouched drink and headed towards the billiards room.

I picked Marconi out immediately. He sat on a bar stool, drink in hand, between two pretty women. He wore a white dress shirt, dark casual slacks, and expensive loafers on his slender frame. Heavy gold jewelry adorned his skinny neck, ear, and wrist, the weight of which would have put him at risk of drowning in a deep body of water. I almost laughed at the gold cross lying on his chest. The most questionable of characters threw a cross around their neck as if it would absolve them of their sins. He chuckled, his pencil thin mustache to crest, as two large brutes, apparently members of his support staff, attempted to play pool. They came to attention on my approach.

"Mr. Marconi?"

"Who are you?" He sneered and studied my wardrobe.

"I'm Jack. I called yesterday."

He smiled and held out his hand. "Joey Marconi." He said it mechanically like he enjoyed hearing the rhyme in his voice. He got up from the stool. "Excuse me, girls."

He put a hand on my shoulder. "Let's go outside." He motioned to the pool players who put the cue sticks down and began to follow us back to the rear bar entrance.

I stopped and glanced at his two sidekicks. "Hey Joey, this is real embarrassing for me. I'd prefer not to have an audience."

Joey examined me for a moment and nodded to the largest of the bodyguards. "Check him." The man started toward me before Joey grabbed him by the shirt. "Not here in front of everyone, you idiot." Joey motioned with his head back towards the billiards room. We retreated back to the room where the bruiser patted me down and announced, "He's clean."

Joey nodded. "Okay Jack, let's go." He turned. "You guys go back to the game. I'll call if I need you." I marveled at his self-assurance and wished I could feel the same. Had his bodyguards escorted us, I would have had to abandon my plan or things would have gotten ugly.

We went through the back door into the parking lot. "Where is she?"

"She's passed out in the backseat of my car."

"Perfect. We can pull up a vehicle and drop her right inside."

We walked to the car and he peered inside. He whistled. "She's got some body. No wonder you was cheatin' on your wife. I woulda gotten rid of the wife."

"Too expensive."

"I hear ya. You got the cash?"

"In the glove compartment." I opened the passenger door and the light went on. A glance back confirmed Joey's preoccupation with Jesse's legs, now exposed all the way to her rose-colored thong panties revealing the majority of her left butt cheek. I had counted on his being distracted by the view, as I removed my gun left in the glove compartment in anticipation of them frisking me.

"Here you go."

Joey continued to peer intently through the rear window despite the promise of the 5K. He finally turned and found the muzzle of my gun in his face. "You yell and I'll smash your face. The girls won't like that." I grabbed him by his shirt collar, pulling him over behind the dumpster under a light on the corner of the adjacent building. I turned him around and pushed him against the wall, patted him down, and removed a gun from his belt, tossing it into the dumpster.

"You're a dead man." Marconi raged. The veins in his neck bulged.

"Not if I kill you first. I'm going to make this really easy for you. I have a picture of a girl. You tell me where she is and I leave you alone." Holding the gun on him, I pulled the picture of Sarah from my suit pocket, and handed it to him so he could see it under the light. He turned and studied the photo.

"Yeah, I remember her. Pretty little thing. Messed up like your girlfriend, if that's a true story. I sold her to a pimp in L.A."

"You gotta name?"

"I'll tell you, but he'll torture and kill you before you get near her. He'll probably do the same to me."

"Name."

"He goes by the nickname 'Junky'." The name made my stomach clutch and bile rise to my throat. My knees buckled with the memory, the gun wavered in my hand. Joey noticed. "Yeah, you know who I'm talkin' about, don't you? You're making a big mistake."

My instincts told me to get out of there fast. I backed off while still holding the gun on him until I reached the car. Joey started moving for the back door as I slid in and started the car. "Stay down, Jesse."

I backed up, swung the car around in the parking lot, and accelerated out onto 4th street just as Joey's thugs were exiting the back door into the parking lot. Joey was yelling to them and an image of them running and pulling out their guns flashed across the rearview mirror as the car squealed through a right turn onto 4th street. Punching the gas, I yelled again for Jesse to stay down as a bullet winged the sideview mirror and a pop from a second bullet took out a rear light. The speedometer hit 65 as I headed for downtown and my office. They didn't seem to be following, but I wasn't taking any chances. "Are you okay, Jesse?"

Silence greeted my question. I panicked. "Jesse, are you all right?" I turned on the interior light and could see her in the rearview mirror sitting upright in the back seat, a angry gaze in her eyes. As we approached I-40, I turned onto Frontage Road, and cruised into the back end of a busy Lowe's parking area and killed the lights. I jumped out of the car just as she emerged from the back door and attempted to catch me with a right hook. I caught her hand balled into a fist. I slowly brought her arms down and wrapped mine around her. After about 30 seconds. I could feel the tension release in her body and the distant gaze dissipate from her eyes. As she recovered, I let go of her arms and she reached around and held me close, her head dropping to my shoulder. She smelled of sweet lavender and her soft, short blonde bangs tickled my nostrils. I didn't move.

We released each other, her face only inches from mine. The urge to feel and taste her lips and tongue overwhelmed me. I peered into her hazel eyes "Did you have one of your spells?"

"Yes, I'm sorry. They were shooting at us."

"Yeah, they're nice guys." I led her by the hand to the front of the car and opened the door so she could crawl into the front seat. "You're sure you're okay?"

She saw my concern and smiled. "I'm fine now, really."

I got in and started the car. She reached over and grabbed my right arm. "I heard what he said. You know this Junky? He's the one that has Sarah?"

"Yeah, I know him. Every cop in L.A. knows him." I sighed. "We have a history." I drove to my apartment and parked the Chrysler in the neighboring apartment's lot. We walked to my place, got my car, and drove to my office. Would Joey try to track me down or leave the violence up to Junky? Regardless, Jesse needed to be safely out of town in case there were any violent repercussions.

I told Jesse about Junky on the drive to the office. "I had been on the force for about a year when we busted him the first time. We had an airtight case but his lawyer had him out in three days. Being inexperienced and naïve about how things worked, I believed you built up your case against a criminal and they went to jail. We had clear evidence of his running drugs and prostitution rings all across the city, plus a lot of circumstantial evidence he or his employees had killed women who thought they could sever their professional relationship with him."

"And you're going to L.A. to confront this guy?" She sounded worried.

"I don't have a choice. He has Sarah."

"Why not just contact the police?"

"I don't trust the police. The visit needs to be a surprise. If Junky gets wind of what I'm after they'll kill Sarah and then come after me." We reached my building and after checking the street, we left the car and hustled inside to my office. I pulled down the window shades and turned on a desk lamp. It had an adjustable glass cover that tilted away from the windows to reduce the potential of our shadows being visible from the outside.

Jesse leaned over with her hands resting on the desk. "You have anything to drink in here?"

I reached into my desk drawer, pulled out a bottle of Jack Daniels, and filled each glass with a healthy shot. We sat on my small sofa. The booze lubricated my gut, settled my nerves, and loosened my tongue. I told her most of the rest of the story.

"It wasn't until several years after Junky's first bust that I suspected my fellow cops were involved in the prostitution ring. I anticipated some pay offs and corruption, but not the depth of the conspiracy committed by my partner and his cohorts."

"Couldn't you go to your supervisor or someone at a higher level and report your suspicions?"

"Not really. They had enough brass on the take to head off any investigation attempt. I wanted to bust these crooked cops, but I was afraid of losing my job, my life, and the lives of my wife and kid."

Jesse sipped her drink and stared right at me. "Did you take any bribes?"

"No, but by not saying anything I was an accessory. As the pressure mounted, my consumption of booze increased after work just so I could go home and sleep for a few hours. Drinking waged an increasingly intense war on my conscience. It corrupted my sense of morality, and contributed to my failure as a husband and father."

"What happened to your family?"

"During my suspension and while the investigation proceeded, my wife resigned her job with the medical examiner's office and disappeared with my daughter. The marriage was pretty much dead by then, and my indictment proved to be the nails in the shut coffin. Being around the law enforcement community, Joanne knew what to expect. Despite my destructive habits and outward indifference, my kid means the world to me. Joanne sensed the danger and got our daughter out of there."

Jesse nodded. "Smart woman. So what happened next?"

"After the case leaked to the media and became a public embarrassment to the department, Internal Affairs arrived to investigate. A dozen cops, me included, received temporary suspensions while the investigation proceeded. I dreaded being interrogated knowing the other cops would exact vengeance if they suspected me of whistle blowing. I hadn't told anyone about what I knew, but several of the cops were suspicious."

I glanced at Jesse as we sipped our drinks, but her blank expression revealed nothing about what she thought about me. No one knew the entire story, not even my ex-wife. The pressure to unload the story had been building inside for so long.

"Have you spoken to her? I mean your daughter."

"Not in over a year."

Jesse nodded sympathetically. "Go on."

"Despite being hurt and embarrassed, my dad stepped in and helped me hire a lawyer."

"Why was he embarrassed?"

"He's a former cop and he just assumed I was guilty."

"How sad. So what did you do?"

"I stayed home with a new security system and reinforced locks on the doors and windows. My Smith & Wesson became my new mate, replacing my wife on the pillow next to me. Peeking through the window shades, I occasionally saw fellow officers drive by in their private vehicles. To leave the house, I snuck out through the backyard or called a cab and dashed to the curb. Like in the movie *Serpico*, I was convinced someone had rigged my car with a bomb."

"You must have been terrified. But they didn't kill you."

"Despite the official warning placed on us not to communicate with each other, I called my partner after a few weeks and described the hell my life had become. I should have won an Oscar for my role as the innocent bystander. Benny promised relief and within a week, the harassing phone calls and daily drive-bys stopped. My partner had explained to the other suspended cops that I didn't know enough to implicate any of them and they were actually drawing attention to themselves by harassing an honest cop. I appreciated my partner running interference for me, but I never forgave him for putting my family in such danger."

"So, eventually you had to testify."

"My deposition provided little detail to Internal Affairs. I maintained an aura of ignorance and responded to the cross-examination without misstep. In the end, most of the cops were acquitted due to a lack of evidence. I suspected I.A. never put much effort into the investigation given the number of cops involved and the possibility the bribes had reached higher levels in the bureaucracy. After nearly six months of investigation, three cops, having been particularly careless, were fired for professional indiscretion. Someone had to take the fall to prevent the media from paying too much attention to the waste of taxpayer's money. Four months later, I sold the house and resigned after a six-year career."

We sat quietly for a long time. The confession had exhausted me. Jesse studied me for a moment. "So how did you end up in Albuquerque?"

"I didn't know where to go. I grew up in Phoenix, but it was too close to L.A. My wife and daughter were gone and my Arizona family had abandoned me. I knew Andy had quit his job as a deputy sheriff with L.A. County and moved back to New Mexico. He invited me to visit, so I packed up the car with what little I had left and departed for Albuquerque. I stayed with Andy for a few months and he gave me work assisting him with some cases. He never asked for a dime, even though I had some money after making a small profit on the house. Eventually, I rented an apartment and landed a few cases on my own; mostly from wives or husbands who wanted me to determine whether their spouses were cheating."

"Where are your wife and daughter?"

"Not sure exactly, but I suspect Joanne is in Vegas. Her sister lives there."

She started to ask another question, but I interrupted. "Please Jesse, I'd feel a lot better with you back in Santa Fe."

She nodded and stood up. "I do need to go." She walked over and opened the door. She stopped and turned to me. "I like you, Arch. You're a nice guy."

"I like you too, Jesse." She gave me an inscrutable smile guys find hard to interpret. The kind that maybe represented a heartfelt declaration of attraction or also could have been dismissed as a "thanks for your efforts." Just about the time I marshaled the courage for a clever retort, she was out the office door. The tenderness had lasted for only a blissful second, but it meant something, didn't it? I locked my office door and hurried after her.

I stopped her at the building doorway to scan the street. It looked clear, but as we exited, I kept one hand on the gun in my belt and one hand on her arm, ready to move us quickly if I saw a car coming down the street at this time of the night. Her admission that she liked me triggered my false bravado.

We stopped at her car. "You okay to drive?"

"I'll be fine." She smiled and opened her eyes wide to reassure me. She opened her car door as I scanned the street. She turned to me. "Be careful in L.A." She gave me a quick peck on the lips and drove off.

CHAPTER 12

A rush hour traffic jam on the I-10 just before the Santa Monica Freeway welcomed me back to the City of Angels. Finally, I arrived at the airport to drop off my car and pick up a rental as a precaution. My ex-colleagues might recognize my conspicuous bright yellow New Mexico license plate with "UCLA" followed by "88", my number for three years of varsity football.

I returned to the terminal to find a payphone near the baggage claim area. I dialed the number for the LAPD Pacific Station in Culver City where my ex-partner Benny McAllister had been reassigned after his acquittal in the scandal. My watch read 5:15 p.m. Benny worked the day shift and most likely had departed—I didn't intend to speak to him, but needed to determine if he'd left for the day. He didn't need to know about my arrival in L.A. until later that evening. The dispatcher informed me Officer McAllister was no longer on duty. I thanked her and hung up.

At the first island in front of the terminal, I caught the shuttle bus to the Enterprise car rental facility, where I picked a Cadillac DTS. The car was big enough to seat the entire UCLA offensive line, and also had an eight-cylinder engine should a fast getaway be necessary.

I headed north on Sepulveda before turning west onto Lincoln and into Playa Del Rey. The parking lot of Outlaws featured an enormous marquee of an art deco cowboy, presumably of the law breaking variety, leaning back and hoisting a frosted mug overloaded with beer suds. The cowboy hovered above me as I headed for the wooden stairs and deck as darkness descended upon the coast. A thick fog settled in, chilling the air. The ocean smell was comforting, but the cold humidity, so rare in my new desert home, penetrated my light jacket and sent me indoors with the other patrons.

I checked for Benny in the dimly lit main bar and in The Library, a room where groups ate dinner at tables surrounded by bookshelf-lined walls filled with the classics.

With no sign of my ex-partner, I settled on a bar stool and ordered a Pyramid. Jeanie, the cute, plump bartender flashed a smile. Did she remember me from the old days?

Despite my recent absence, a similar cast of characters assembled at the bar. A man with dark shades wearing a blue wool sweater under a camel-haired coat sat across from me. Without checking, I knew his seeing-eye dog was nestled at the man's feet, his butt against the bar and his body lying forward through the legs of the barstool. Gordy, an old friend of Benny's, had owned and operated Gordon's Market, a small grocery across the street from the bar. His gray hair had thinned considerably and he wore ragged pants the color of a California tangerine. His wife had passed away and without her guidance, getting dressed must have been like playing fashion Russian roulette.

After about an hour, a stool opened up next to Gordy. As I sat, Gordy's head tilted toward me.

"Hello Gordy."

"Hmm, I recognize the voice. Don't tell me." He hesitated as if his memory was trying to catch up with his hearing. "Well keep talking, damnit. I can't guess if you're silent."

"You mean my aura isn't strong enough for you to recognize me, you old coot?"

Gordy smiled. "Arch? Arch Caldwell, is that you?"

"The one and only."

"Where you been?"

"Albuquerque."

"Isn't that on the other side of Arizona in Mexico?" Gordy broke out in a low rumbling laughter that fell into a hacking cough. He never had much patience for geographically- challenged people and he let anyone in the bar know if they slipped up. His blindness gave him carte blanche when it came to being rude, especially with complete strangers. People said things in front of Gordy, they wouldn't have said in the presence of a person with full sight. It was a strange phenomenon, the blindness created a sense of security, as if the lack of vision dulled the other senses. Well positioned in his store or on a stool in the bar, he became a listening post, picking up individual conversations normally buried in the aural layers reverberating in a crowded room.

He had been a great source of tips during my LAPD days.

Gordy recovered and took a sip of his beer. "What you doin' here?"

"I'm looking for Benny."

He tilted his head in my direction. "He know you lookin' for him?"

"Not yet. I just got into town."

"Haven't talked to him tonight. Might've gone home."

"It would be a first if he went home before stopping at Outlaws."

Gordy threw his head back, letting out a short snort. "Aint it the truth, Arch."

His bottle of Budweiser had a few sips of beer left. I motioned to Jeanie. "Can I get another Bud here for my friend Gordy?"

She nodded, dove into the silver ice chest, and came out with the familiar red bottle delivered open with a smack on the wood in front of Gordy. He guzzled what remained in the old bottle, which Jeanie promptly removed.

"Mighty kind of you, Arch." I tapped his bottle with my empty one, prompting me to order another Pyramid.

After taking a healthy swig, Gordy turned slightly, his face angled toward me. "You got a bum deal, Arch."

"How's that Gordy?"

"You was implicated in that scandal, but I know for a fact you wasn't guilty of anything."

"How can you be so sure?"

"I know these things." He tapped his forehead just above the sunglasses.

"Yeah, well you're right most of the time. There was never anything wrong with your hearing or memory."

He nodded, leaned toward my beer, and took an exaggerated sniff. "You drinking wheat beer now?"

"Sure. You still smelling beer for a living, Gordy?"

Gordy had made a lot of money over the years betting visitors he could guess what kind of beer they were drinking. That would encourage the strangers to silently order one of the more obscure brands. With his keen sense of smell, and memory of the hundred or so beers served in the joint, he could guess the correct beer 99% of the time with just one sniff. It provided good entertainment and Gordy enjoyed impressing the gullible participants with his skills as he separated them from their money. The bolder losers challenged Gordy, thinking it was a scam, but a quick removal of those shades convinced any doubter. Gordy's eyes resembled pool cue balls—the empty white sheen of a man who had not seen the light of day in an entire lifetime.

I always wondered why Gordy's keen senses did not apply to taste, since he now chose to drink Bud rather than any of the many varieties of beer available. Perhaps he wasn't willing to spend the extra buck.

Gordy's advanced olfactory senses impressed me. Having similar skills made Andy Lujan such a good detective. He used to guess the brand of colognes and perfumes of customers passing our table while we dined in a restaurant. Feelings of sorrow and loss drifted past like small clouds crossing in front of the sun.

Gordy's eyebrows arched upwards. "You okay, Arch?"

"Sure, Gordy. Just thinking about all the good times here in L.A."

"Yeah, right."

We drank in silence until I finished my beer. "Let me give you my phone number Gordy, just in case you see Benny."

"Sure, Arch." He pulled a black smartphone out of his pants and slid it on the bar in front of me. "Just state your name followed by your number. It will be saved automatically in my contact list."

"You getting all high-tech on me, Gordy?"

"Unfortunately, some of us with disabilities have to rely on such gadgets. You're lucky."

"Everybody's got some kind of disability, Gordy. You've adapted better than most."

"Maybe you're right, Arch." He tipped his bottle towards mine and I toasted him with my empty one.

I followed his instructions and entered my name and number before placing the smartphone on the bar on front of him with a soft clunk so he knew it was there. He nodded and returned the phone to his pants pocket.

I left Gordy with another Bud and headed back to my car around 9:00 p.m. Gordy would alert Benny of my return should he arrive later, but he was a happy-hour drinker and rarely visited at this hour.

For most cops then and now, happy hour provided a daily transition from the law enforcement mentality that consumed us before we headed home to family, a lover, or an empty apartment. After Benny's three kids graduated and moved away, he tried to return home to his wife at a reasonable hour. Despite being a crooked, mediocre cop, he'd been a committed husband and father.

Heading to the bar after every shift made me feel like a rebellious teenager. The social networking helped build camaraderie with my fellow officers, but left the full responsibility of raising our child to my wife. Over time, my alcohol dependency took such a firm hold only the shock of a complete breakdown stopped me at the brink of destruction.

Leaving L.A. had saved me, but for what I wasn't certain. With those ponderous thoughts, I headed downtown to find a hooker.

CHAPTER 13

I exited at 3rd Street and cut back underneath the expressway to Figueroa, where the less classy prostitutes worked in the shadow of the high-rises and highway underpasses. I cruised along, looking for Paula, a prostitute with whom I'd once had a non-sexual professional relationship. Her leads had assisted me in breaking open several cases, although I lost her trust after getting embroiled in an investigation to bring down her pimp.

Paula could have been working the higher-class Hollywood area. She was pretty. I hoped to get a glimpse of her or one of the other girls who would know where to find her. Seeing a familiar figure, I pulled over in front of a tall woman with ebony skin and massive breasts spilling out of her white halter-top. She wore thin, tight red pants that left little imagination as to what the client would be buying.

When I pulled up and rolled the window down, she came over and leaned in, the impact of her breasts in the seat cavity should have set off the passenger-side airbag. "Hi Casey."

It took a second for the recognition to register. "Holy shit, man. You ain't been around in a while."

"Yeah. I don't live in town anymore and I no longer work for LAPD. I'm looking for Paula. Have you seen her around tonight?"

"No, man. I think she over working in the 'wood' area."

"Okay, thanks. Here's my card just in case I miss her. It has my cell number. I'd appreciate it if you give it to her and ask her to call me."

She read the card and laughed. "You a private dick now?"

"Yeah, good one Casey. Please give that to her."

She nodded and lifted her chest from the car, easing my claustrophobia. She was getting up there in age, and I wondered what would happen to her when she could no longer turn tricks. Her rough life had begun to show. There would be no 401K plan offered by her boss, a man I had unsuccessfully tried to put away. I had a lot of respect for women like Casey. They risked their lives every day like the cops on the beat. Most of the women had no other way to pay the bills.

I drove through some of the familiar little ethnic neighborhoods I worked as a young officer out of the LAPD Olympic Street Station. Chinatown, Filipinotown, Little Bangladesh, Koreatown— the streets adorned with pawnshops, cheap hotels, auto repair shops, and questionable hole-in-the wall eating establishments. I looked for a familiar one identified by a neon sign poised over the corner of Olympic and Vermont. I'd eaten there a few times before and it had a good chance of not giving me food poisoning.

I found the Singing Palace and parked in the alley out back. I'm not sure how it got its name, but I didn't care as long as my stomach didn't launch into a heavy metal concert after eating the food. I donned a Dodgers baseball cap, and walked out of the alley to the main intersection to peer into the window. I wanted to make sure no former colleagues were present. Since not all the tables were in view, thanks to a wall of fake plants and a large aquarium filled with exotic fish, I had to accept the risk.

The dark lobby, lit by a tall black floor lamp and the bulb of the aquarium, featured an antique cash register resting on a glass case filled with gums and candies. The place smelled like fried fish. The owner came over and immediately recognized me as an important customer despite my prolonged absence. He led me to a table, but I asked for a booth in the shadowy corner away from the window.

The owner's wife made a joyful production out of seeing me again as she handed me a menu. My last meal had been somewhere in Arizona. Hunger spasms now rocked me. The enticing aromas like the siren voices of Greek mythology lured me to my potential culinary peril.

I ordered a familiar dish: the mixed vegetable Udon soup with thin strips of mystery meat floating among the broccoli, cabbage, and bean sprouts. I bet on the boiling of the soup to kill any potent intestinal invaders. The flavor proved to be delicious and I headed through Little Tokyo satiated by the warm broth.

I drove down Spring Street past City Hall Park and scanned the streets for Paula. I parked in the lot across from The Edison, a former power plant built in 1910, now a modern-day speakeasy located in the basement of the historic Higgins Building. I deposited my gun into the glove compartment and added a jacket and tie to my outfit.

Luckily, there was no line to get in. The bouncer admitted me after a quick glance at my attire. I descended into a dark gothic industrial interior and walked through a brick-canyon hallway to the main bar. I ordered a Chimay White beer at the bar that wrapped itself around the length of the red and brown brick wall like a coiled copper snake. The shine on the polished redwood bar surface was crisp enough to see my reflection. The recessed lighting in the high ceiling doused the walls and highlighted the white mortar.

A modest crowd of well-dressed men and women gathered in small groups. I had only been to the club once, but it had a reputation for attracting the most enticing escorts in the city. With no sign of Paula, I searched the rest of the building, passing through a large open cathedral space with leather couches and chairs tucked into dark corners—the only light came from tall elaborate candelabra chandeliers. Another room contained the original power plant generator. I dodged the people sitting on assorted ottomans scattered across the floor. The walls included sketches of burlesque dancers. There seemed to be an endless number of rooms, many small, dark, and dingy. I managed to find my way back to the main bar. No sign of Paula. She could be turning a trick at this late hour, making her return to the club unlikely.

I returned to my car and circled the neighborhood. Paula's unmistakable contours appeared ahead on 2nd Street—her shapely frame, and long black hair tied into two long pigtails slid all the way down to the top of her short colorful paisley skirt. The tie-dyed blouse, bunched in a knot at her sternum, exposed her flat stomach. She resembled a psychedelic Judy Garland from Wizard of Oz. Apparently done for the night, she shopped the windows of several closed vintage clothing stores.

A handful of quarters deposited in a meter slot bought me about an hour of parking time. I popped a stick of gum in my mouth and hustled back down to where she stood outside a jewelry store.

"Hey gorgeous. How about I buy you some ice-cream?"

She turned and screamed, "Arch. Oh my God." I received a kiss on the cheek and she held me at arms-length. "I haven't seen you since....I don't know how long."

"How are you Paula? Are you staying healthy?"

"Of course. Why wouldn't I? You serious about buying me some ice-cream?" She released me and smiled.

"Absolutely. You done for the night?"

"Yes, I did good. I left Fig Street permanently. Much nicer clientele around here and I can charge more, which makes you-know-who happy." She stepped closer and lightly brushed my cheek with her hand.

I held her hand. "I'm glad. It wasn't safe around there."

"I know. We lost several girls this year, probably murdered. We need you back on the force, Arch."

I laughed. "Not likely. And I didn't have much success anyway."

"Not for lack of trying. Wow, I can't believe it's you." She slipped her arm inside mine and we walked the three blocks back toward downtown like lovers out for a late evening stroll. It was nice to have some female companionship, even from a friend who happened to be a prostitute.

"You like my costume?"

"Yes, I can hear the sitar from "Strawberry Fields" ringing in my head."

She punched me in the arm. "Oh, Arch. I've missed you."

We made it to the Mikawaya Ice Cream Parlor a few minutes before it closed. A car swung by and honked several times before continuing down the street. It rattled my nerves until I saw it wasn't the Hummer Paula's boss and my former nemesis drove. I wasn't ready for my encounter with him.

"One of your customers?"

"Probably, I don't care. I like being with you, Arch. You know you wouldn't have to pay." She squeezed my arm.

"Thanks, Paula. But I think of you as a friend."

She glanced up at me with a tired smile. "I know. I had several clients tonight."

I nodded my understanding. Even if willing, I figured the last thing she needed was another man inside her. She was a pretty woman whose full lips, penetrating eyes, and light complexion would tempt most men. Perhaps if things were different I might have been attracted to her, but her being a prostitute was difficult for me to overcome.

"I like having you as a friend, Arch. I heard your wife left you during the investigation."

"Yeah, she moved to Vegas with Josie."

Paula hugged my arm tighter. "She obviously didn't appreciate you."

"No, Paula. It was the other way around. I didn't appreciate what I had enough to clean up my act."

"Is it too late?"

"I'm afraid it is."

She pulled me in through the doorway of the shop. "Come on, we could both use some ice cream."

The bright track lighting inside the ice cream parlor nearly blinded me as we peered at the variety of frozen treats in the chest freezers. The fresh iced smell drifted through a slit at the bottom of the glass case. She ordered a chocolate hazelnut mochilato, and I opted for the mango ice cream mochi. We sat at one of the small square cafeteria tables.

"You gonna tell me why you came back? I know this isn't a social call."

"A guy hired me to find his daughter." I pulled the picture of Sarah from my jacket pocket and showed it to her. She took it with her other hand moving the ice-cream cone away from it. She rotated the picture trying to maximize the overhead lighting to get the best view.

"Whew. She's a doll, but young."

"She's seventeen and I think Junky has her. I was hoping you might recognize her."

She peered at me intently. "Is this an excuse to go after him again?"

I smiled hoping to convince her that the fury of those days no longer gripped me. "No, those days are over. This is legit. I just want to find the girl and take her home."

"You know it isn't going to be easy."

"I know but I've got a plan."

"I hope it's a good one."

"Hopefully it's good enough. Have you seen her?"

"No, but I hear things."

"You've got the best hearing of anyone I know."

She laughed. "She might be up in Redondo Beach. Junky likes to use the young ones for his more distinguished clients."

"I need to get to Junky before he spots me. Does he have an office up there now?"

"It's hard to say. He moves around a lot, but I know a guy who might be a lead. He's a waiter at Seafood House on the Pier. You know it?"

"Yeah, I've been there a few times."

"His name is Emilio. But you didn't hear it from me, Arch. Seriously, I don't need any shit coming down on me." She grabbed my hand for emphasis.

"I know, Paula. I promise. Junky will never know I got this tip from you. I've always protected you. Nothing's changed."

She tightened her grip on my hands and nodded but without the trusted expression that used to come automatically. I knew she didn't want me upsetting the recent balance and financial stability in her life.

That night I found a cheap hotel near the airport. I had a hard time falling asleep, anticipating the possible confrontation with my ex-partner. Seeing Benny would rekindle bad memories. I resisted going out for a drink as my thoughts turned to my daughter. My catharsis had been rocky, but it might get a boost if I could survive my return to L.A and save another young girl's life.

CHAPTER 14

"Hello Benny. How's my ex-partner?" A prolonged silence on the phone greeted my question. "What? You're not happy to hear my voice after all this time?"

"What do you want?"

"I'm in town and thought we might meet to discuss some business."

"What kind of business?"

"I'll tell you when I see you."

"We've got nothing to discuss."

"Well, that's where you're wrong. I drove all the way to L.A. just to see you and this is the response I get?"

"I'm not meeting you unless you tell me what it's about."

"No can do, my friend. But, I will tell you that ignoring me would not be in your best interest. If you know what I mean?"

"No, I have no idea what you mean."

"Meet me today at the old abandoned car lot below the one-ten overpass. Five o'clock, and don't be late."

"What abandoned car lot?"

"Don't be stupid, Benny. You know exactly what lot I'm talking about." The location had served as a rendezvous spot for Benny and his cronies. They met there in the old days, picking the spot because of its isolation and noise from the passing overhead traffic. A place where important decisions were made and big money exchanged hands. My choice for the meeting place represented my first shot across the wave-battered bow of Benny's comfortable lifestyle.

He agreed to meet me after work. Following his initial indignation, we launched into a banal conversation lobbing false pleasantries tinged with tension. I hung up after warning him again not to be late.

I had no sympathy for Benny. He'd made his own bed, and the truth was my silence had kept him from prison. Despite the suspension and subsequent re-assignment, he must have still been as crooked as the jagged peaks of the Sandia Mountains back home; otherwise, Junky would have had a bullet put in his gut. He probably hoped to coast into a comfortable retirement supported by his illegal activities. But my sudden unwelcome reappearance put his impending solace in jeopardy.

CHAPTER 15

I arrived at the junkyard two hours early and parked my rental car around the corner. The poor, mostly minority neighborhood consisted of decaying houses. The boarded up windows and disrepair suggested abandoned residences. I wondered how many contained hidden meth labs. Rusted trash cans, empty beer bottles, plastic bags, and paper cups littered the street, likely forgotten by the Streets and Sanitation Department.

A lone dog barked from one of the adjacent yards overgrown with weeds. I slipped through a break in the perimeter fence under the whoosh of cars passing overhead on the highway. Signs of the homeless were everywhere. No one knew who owned the junkyard, an inheritance battle had erupted after the death of the previous owner during my LAPD employment. The city threatened for years to foreclose and take ownership, but without the necessary funds, they continued to ignore the property.

The yard's isolation made it an ideal place to conduct shady business. The dirty cops, who valued the location for its privacy, used to run off the homeless to eliminate potential witnesses to their crimes. I had investigated murders of homeless men and local prostitutes, who I suspected had been killed in the junkyard, their bodies dumped elsewhere. Like a dog unwilling to soil its cage, the cops didn't want dead bodies where they conducted their sordid business.

The junkyard reeked of grease, motor oil, and transmission fluid. The engines, carburetors, and radiators had ceased to function long ago. Car hoods stood raised as if in surrender after being scavenged for parts. Toward the old operation center, entropy ensued and the rusted metal carcasses became scattered randomly as if the operator had run out of the patience needed to maintain order. A covey of piled car skeletons, likely the next victims of the compactor when the operator received a pink-slip, sat abandoned next to an old crane that must have dropped the cars into a pit to create steel Rice Krispie bars for transport.

The dilapidated office tower, where I was to meet Benny, hovered behind the crane. Near the tower sat a silver Impala, a model from the 70s, the finish now having faded in the California sunshine to a matte dolphin gray. Leprous rust patches had begun to devour the metal exterior. A tall dump trunk with the driver's side door intact stood next to the Impala, fifty feet from the tower. The higher position of the cab would provide a good vantage point to see Benny's approach across the littered landscape and see if he kept his word about coming alone. The door also faced east so the late afternoon sun would be setting behind me, making it more difficult for Benny to see me in the glare. I suspected the choice of this location had caused him much consternation. He might act irrationally.

On the opposite side of the truck, the passenger door hung like an old scab, dangling from a single rusted hinge. I climbed into the cab, and lying across the black, torn vinyl seat, I kicked the door just below the hinge. The truck frame groaned. After several more strikes, the door ripped loose with a screech and fell to the ground with a soft crash. The driver's door would provide cover, while the open door would allow me to easily disappear into the maze of rusted cars.

I checked the view through the open windowless frame, the glass having been long-ago shattered, the pieces now glimmering amongst the sluggishly decomposing sand, dirt, and human paraphernalia. Amazingly, the still intact rear-view mirror afforded a clear view of the area around the operator's tower from a prone position in the truck. My stomach growled with hunger, but the filth, bird excrement, and rat turds in the cab depressed my appetite. The sickle-shaped remnant of a bird's mud nest clung to the upper corner of the cab where a sun visor had been attached. Small pieces of dried dark brown mud littered the dashboard along with a thick layer of grayish dust. I shivered and stuck my head out the vehicle's window to escape the grime.

I recalled my early days with the LAPD, fresh out of the academy, honored to be teamed with a veteran cop like Benny. He vowed to show me the ropes. He appreciated my eagerness to prove myself, a trait common to many rookie cops. However, it didn't take me long to realize his ropes would have bound me to greed and corruption, a condition I neither accepted nor rejected. My indecision triggered Benny's mistrust. He never confided in me. That probably saved my life.

I checked my weapon and tested my aim perched in the driver's seat. My shooting hand barely shook. The brick lodged in the pit of my stomach since my arrival in L.A. wouldn't go away. I took a deep breath and considered my mission. Retrieve Sarah and get the hell out of town.

A blue BMW eased down the side street followed by a cloud of dust as Benny drove into the junkyard through a large gap in the fence. He slowed and eventually pulled the car in front of the tower. Benny stepped gingerly out of his vehicle and wiped away dust from his navy blue suit and pants. His dark hair had thinned a bit, while his belly had widened a lot since I last saw him. He smoothed his yellow and blue Lakers tie over his white shirt and surveyed the area before walking into the deteriorating tower.

I had slipped down on the cab's seat behind the door. Benny had arrived a half-hour early, most likely to get a jump on me. I wanted him to think he had succeeded.

The tower's wood stairs creaked as Benny climbed. From the rearview mirror, I saw his head poke through the second floor window to search the surroundings. I resisted the temptation to confront him. Maybe he would think I changed my mind.

Benny left the window and I heard him descend the tower's steps. I slipped out the passenger door to crouch behind the Impala's frame and front tire, directly across from Benny's car.

He came out of the tower and headed for his car. His black patent-leather shoes crunched on the crystalized dirt. I stood up from behind the car.

"Hello Benny."

He turned and reached for his gun as I ducked back behind the vehicle. A shot whizzed over the Impala's car hood followed by the sound of his scampering feet.

"Benny, you asshole, it's Arch," I yelled as a second and third bullet careened off metal to my left and right. I was tempted to put a bullet through his shiny driver's side door, payback for all the misery he had caused me.

Benny's feet were visible when I crouched to the ground from behind the Impala's wheel and peered underneath to his car. I had always been a smarter cop than Benny and never would have left my feet exposed. I was also a much better shot. I settled into firing position bracing myself on the ground, aimed, and fired. Benny screamed as I sprinted around the Impala, slid across the hood of his car, and rolled over my left shoulder, landing in perfect firing position. My melodramatic entrance wasn't necessary. Benny had dropped his gun and sat on the ground holding his left foot.

"Jesus Christ, Arch, you shot me." Benny began unlacing his left shoe.

"You shot at me first, you dumb ass."

"I didn't recognize your voice."

"Sure, you didn't recognize your old partner's voice." I got up and walked toward his prone figure with my gun ready. I stopped about five feet away. "You should have known better than to get into a shoot-out with me. Kick your gun away from your body or I'll put a hole in your right foot."

"I'm not going to shoot at you."

"You already did. Just do it." Benny obliged and kicked the gun towards me with his undamaged right foot. I picked up the Beretta 9 mm. "Are you ever going to learn how to use this thing?" I tapped his left leg just above the ankle. "And the model sixty in your ankle holster, Benny. Nice and slow."

He pulled up his pant leg, removed the small frame Smith and Wesson, and tossed it in my direction.

"You thought I forgot about it. It's a good thing you didn't make a move for it because I would have killed you."

"When I get up and reach my radio, I'll have you arrested for shooting a cop."

"Not when you hear what I have to say." I saw the blood ooze onto the ground through the hole in his shoe. "You're lucky I'm accurate. I could have hit you in the ankle. That would have been really painful."

"Fuck you, Arch." He removed his shoe with excruciating effort to inspect the wound.

"We can make this real short, Benny, and then you can go get that wound attended to. Just tell the chief you shot yourself in the foot. He'll certainly believe it."

"Christ, Arch. There's a first aid kit in the trunk with some bandages and tape. I need to dress this wound."

"Where are the keys?"

"They're in the ignition. There's a button to pop the trunk."

I stretched across to the steering wheel and removed the keys. I popped the trunk, retrieved the kit, and handed it to him. He cursed as he poured alcohol on the wound. After the alcohol evaporated, he bandaged the toe with gauze and tape to stop the bleeding.

"It's just a flesh wound. You'll recover."

"What do you want from me anyway?" Benny sat upright and flipped his left shoe through the open window.

"I'm looking for a young girl. I'm pretty sure she's in one of Junky's establishments."

"What does that have to do with me?"

"You've got a professional relationship with him and I need financial support."

"I don't know what you're talking about."

"Don't play dumb. You think I don't know about your history with Junky?"

Benny gave me a dismissive wave. "I can't help you. Go back home. You don't want to mess with Junky anymore. Haven't you suffered enough?"

He was right about the last part. "I don't have a choice. I'm here to find this girl and I'm certain he has her."

Benny shifted uncomfortably and not just because of the toe wound. "Why would he even agree to talk to you?"

I played with him, not quite ready to set the hook. "He's a businessman, right? So I was planning to offer him cash for the girl."

"Good luck with that."

"I don't need luck because you're going to put up the cash."

Benny laughed until he reached for his foot and groaned. "You're crazy Arch. Why should I give Junky money? So you can have some whore?"

"Because if you don't, you're going to jail."

"What the hell are you talking about?"

"How do you think I knew about this place, Benny?"

"It's just a fucking junkyard."

"It's not just an abandoned junkyard. You know as well as anybody. I'm familiar with everything about your operation including what happened here."

"You don't know shit."

"You still have the pocket organizer you carried everywhere with you? The one with all those compartments for credit cards and receipts?"

"No, I got a new one. But I kept the old one as a back-up. Why?"

"You remember the hidden compartment where you kept a spare fifty for an emergency?"

"Yeah, so what?"

"Check it when you get home. I put a bug in there when we were working together."

"You what? I don't believe you. You're bluffing."

I laughed. "I counted on the fact you carried that leather organizer everywhere you went. You cared more about that oversized wallet than you did your wife. I figured one day you'd get shot because you were busy organizing your receipts or business cards. You remember those fiber optic listening devices I ordered so we could wire a couple of Junky's girls?

"What about them?"

"They were small enough to stay hidden. I glued one of them into the zipped compartment below your spare fifty. Take a look when you get home."

"Bullshit, Arch. When did you do that?"

"We were sitting at a gas station over on Sepulveda, and I slipped it in when you left it in the car to go take a shit. You were terrified of dropping it in the toilet. It was too large to fit into your jacket pocket so you left it on your car seat while you went to the bathroom."

"No way." He shook his head as if refusing to believe my betrayal, or perhaps remembering his paranoia of flushing his beloved organizer down the toilet.

"Check when you get home. If you never found the device, it must still be in there. It only lasted a few months, but long enough to collect enough details to put you away for a long time. I've got conversations of payoff negotiations and you're one of the stars. I sat

PETE DAVID

in my car a few hundred feet away and recorded everything. I didn't give it to Internal Affairs in case I needed your cooperation someday. That day has arrived."

The amount of information collected from the bug probably couldn't convict anyone, but as Andy always told me, "It isn't what you know, it's what your enemies think you know." Thanks to Andy, I could add even more details to my blackmail tactics since I had several envelopes of incriminating documents.

Benny still didn't seem convinced—I needed to play my trump card. "I know about your meetings with Shockey."

At the mention of the name, a guilty shadow rolled across Benny's face. His eyes widened and his upper lip trembled.

I went for the kill. "I know about the cash payments, how much you were getting and the frequency. Shockey was your banker."

Shockey wasn't the man's real name, but those of us who followed pro football had seen a close resemblance between him and a tight end who played for the New York Giants and New Orleans Saints. Our guy was a mean bastard who used the fear of violence to shake down local L.A. businesses for kickbacks and then paid off the cops to ignore him. He had been a close associate of Junky's in prostitution and drug dealerships. Shockey had paid the price, sacrificed by Junky and the cops, and now served 15 years for attempted bribery and corruption. He never squealed to the authorities about what he knew, perhaps fearing the long reach his former business partners had inside the pen. I looked forward to the fireworks when he got out.

"You son of a bitch, Arch. I protected you when the other cops wanted to kill you."

"You took your sweet time about it. Don't think I'm not appreciative. It's why I haven't divulged the existence of the CD to anyone."

"What CD?"

I continued with my bluff. "I made a greatest hits recording of you and your pals' transactions. It's quite a collection and I'm sure it would be a best seller with the FBI." I could have made a CD, but the barely audible taped conversations would never have held up in court.

"Yeah right. I still don't believe you." He said with little conviction.

"You will when you get home. I needed an insurance policy because there was no way I could trust any of you."

Benny fell silent. If he got home and didn't find any device in his organizer, he could send someone to kill me. Finally, he squinted up at me. "So let's say I believe your story about the CD. What do you want from me?"

"You're going to pay Junky cash for the girl. I was planning to offer him fifteen thousand. Think he'll take it?"

"He might just have you shot."

"That's where you come in."

"What do you mean?"

"You always underestimated my intelligence, Benny. I made a copy of the CD and left it with my attorney in Albuquerque. If I should die for any reason, even natural causes, the CD gets sent to the FBI. You better hope I live a long life and you better convince Junky not to kill me. If he wants more you'll just have to pay him."

"You think I have that kind of money lying around?"

"I know you've got some stashed away where your wife won't find it. You better find the cash." Andy's files had listed numerous bank accounts, but I didn't know which accounts belonged to Benny. If pressed I could rattle off some names and locations, an option I hoped to avoid because if they didn't pertain to Benny, he would suspect a bluff.

"This must be a special girl to make you take such a risk, Arch. Who is she?"

"It's none of your business. You just need to make sure I get out of L.A. alive with her."

"Shit Arch, Junky might just have both of us killed."

I shrugged. "Maybe. But if you hang me out to dry and I get knocked off, you're going to spend the rest of your life in jail."

"What are you going to do?"

"First, I find her. Then confront Junky. If he calls you, it means he hasn't killed me yet. It's up to you to convince him to accept my offer."

"And then what?" The resignation registered on his face.

"Once I leave town with the girl, I'll be out of your life. Hopefully forever, unless my health suddenly fails. In which case, you'll be hearing from the FBI."

Benny pulled himself up using the hood of this car and checked his foot. The bandages had stopped the bleeding. "You're going to get us both shot in the head for sure."

"Then you won't have to worry about going to jail." I scattered the bullets from Benny's guns among the junkyard dust, then tossed the weapons out into the sea of cars.

"Don't let me down, Benny." I hurried out of the junkyard and down the side street, relieved to see the rental car still there. I drove straight to the airport, with a close eye on my rearview mirror. I dropped off the rental and retrieved my car.

I drove over to a Best Western on Manchester near the airport, pulled around to the rear parking area, and backed into a parking space along the row of first floor hotel rooms. My plate was now hidden from view just in case Benny tried to pull a double-cross, and the police got lucky locating my car. I doubted he would want to announce my presence, considering my possession of such damaging information. I thought about renting another car, but I might need to make a quick exit out of town. It wouldn't be safe to take another trip to the airport.

I collapsed in the room and reviewed my confrontation with Benny. His discovery of the dead listening device would secure his cooperation, but wouldn't guarantee his dependability. He was a coward. I hoped his fear of going to jail would secure his focus on the task. On the other hand, Benny was a lucky son of a bitch, and his run of good fortune might continue if he ratted me out and Junky killed me before I turned over the evidence.

CHAPTER 16

A long, welcome shower cleansed me of the dirt and smell of the junkyard. I dressed in a nice suit and headed south on the 405, then east to the coast in Redondo Beach. I pulled into the parking garage at the Redondo pier just as a thick layer of cool fog covered the city in an ethereal blanket. I slipped on my clear glasses, climbed the steps to the pier, and searched for the Seafood House neon sign.

The main door spilled into a small reception corridor, but veered right through another door into the crowded bar. I found an empty seat in a ring of chairs circling a burning fire. The warmth brought a satisfying comfort after walking through the cold Pacific mist. The restaurant smelled of freshly baked bread and grilled fish.

I sipped a rum and coke, and shifted my chair to observe the scurrying staff. There was only one male staff member waiting on tables, so identifying the Hispanic Emilio proved to be easy. I tracked which tables he served, ordered another drink, and waited for the dinner crowd to thin.

The bar seemed like a good place to hang out. It overflowed with raucous drinking customers. I got caught up in the mood and consumed several more drinks for courage. I paid the bar tab and approached the hostess, who seated me at one of Emilio's tables by the window. He came by a minute later and introduced himself. I ordered a glass of ice water and the halibut.

Through the window, I could see the waves crashing on the shore illuminated by the floodlights from the roof. Like a silent movie, no sound penetrated the sealed window. The halibut, delivered fresh from the ice-cold waters of Alaska, was delicious. My last meal at this restaurant had been with Joanne at the beginning of our initial case against Junky. Josie had been born, the job still full of excitement before the stress of the case began to wear me down.

We had initiated a series of sting operations to bust prostitutes hoping they would provide testimony against Junky and put him out of business. We turned several hookers who complained about abuse, and threats of violence.

The case took several years before the District Attorney felt confident of a successful prosecution. Despite police protection, the first of our star witnesses turned up murdered a few days before the court hearing. This prompted a second witness to slip past the cops and disappear. The body of a third witness turned up in the junkyard. Of course, at the time I didn't realize the significance of the location as a meeting place and Junky's selection of it as a warning shot to those cops he had corrupted. With so much gullible emphasis on making a name for myself in the law enforcement community, I was blind to the corruption surrounding me. But, after the murders of those women, my suspicions began to mount.

Without a breathing witness and despite our best efforts to develop the case, it fell apart for lack of sufficient evidence. I spent months in a frenzy trying to track down the one remaining witness who had disappeared before Junky's deadly tentacles reached out to snag her. When pieces of crucial evidence disappeared from a locked room at police headquarters, the depth of corruption became obvious. Not knowing which cops could be trusted, I began conducting my investigations in secrecy.

Linking Junky to the killings proved difficult since he delegated his dirty work. His hands were clean, but plenty of dirt had accumulated under his fingernails. Despite my diligence and strong leads, he would slither through my fingers and escape like a live eel just as my hands tightened around him.

As the difficulties in the prosecution mounted, the decision-makers distanced themselves, focusing on solving easier cases to support their promotions to a comfortable job in the mayor's office. No one cared about murdered prostitutes. The murders cleaned up the streets.

Emilio brought me the bill and I slid my credit card into the folder. He returned, reaching to pick up the bill, but I put my hand down on it to prevent him from escaping.

"Emilio, I'm interested in some late night entertainment and someone told me you're the man to see."

He eyed me suspiciously. "What kind of entertainment you looking for?"

"A companion. Blonde and young. Not too young. I don't want anyone illegal, if you know what I mean."

His blank stare gave me no acknowledgement he understood my request. "Male or female."

It hadn't occurred to me either sex would be offered, but it made sense. Junky wanted to make money and as a savvy businessman he would cater to his client's particular tastes.

"Female. Sorry, I should have specified." I pushed my glasses up on my nose and gave him my best sheepish grin to demonstrate how inexperienced I was at this sort of thing.

"Wait here." He left with a condescending sigh. I sat there for an uncertain eternity before he returned.

A waitress lingered at an adjacent table, gathering dirty dishes as Emilio held my gaze. "Can I get you anything else?"

It sounded like he was dismissing me until he glanced furtively at the waitress, still within hearing range. After she left, he nodded at the bill folder. "Place three hundred dollars in with your bill in one minute." He walked away.

I extracted three of the six, hundred dollar bills from my wallet. What a bargain—I had anticipated it costing me more. I kept the bill folder just above my lap and kept my body turned toward the window to reduce the chance of being observed sliding the bills inside. I placed the bill folder back on the table. Like a falcon Emilio silently swooped in to remove it.

He returned with my credit card poking out the top of the bill folder with a hotel key card and a note, "Royal Suites Hotel, Room 345" tucked inside. I signed the bill, returned the credit card to my wallet, and nervously left the restaurant. The hotel was located on the right side of Harbor Drive, a five-minute drive from the restaurant.

I entered the hotel parking lot and descended into the garage just past the brightly lit hotel entrance. I removed the picture of Sarah from my jacket pocket. Junky would have an entourage of young blonde girls, so it would be sheer luck if the one I paid for turned out to be Sarah. But, the girls knew each other and I had plenty of cash for the right information.

The elevator carried me up to the lobby. The wide space was elegantly lit with a multitude of recessed lights in the ceiling. I noted where all the stairways were located before returning to the elevators. I went up to the third floor. The sign on the intersecting wall indicated room 345 was down the hallway to my right.

The thick carpet muted the sound of my steps in the quiet corridor. A brief muffled sound bite from a television broadcast came from one of the rooms I passed. Room 345 was at the end of the hallway. After a glance back up the hallway, I slipped the card into the slot. A green light and a soft click alerted me that the key worked. I turned the knob and pushed the door open. In the hallway light, the outline of a king-sized bed was visible inside the large bedroom that contained a doorway leading to a bathroom. I pushed the hall door fully open. A mirrored closet stood to my left. The remaining room corridor remained in darkness except for a dim light at the end where a sofa and two chairs faced the mounted TV. I pressed a light switch on the wall next to the door. No light came on.

"Hello." I called out as my conscious hoisted a red warning flag.

"Come on back, honey." A woman's soft voice and a whiff of expensive perfume invited me to enter.

I stepped into the room, but held the door open. A lamp stood on a bedside table on the far side of the bed. I memorized a route to the lamp, stepped forward and let the door close behind me. The room plunged into darkness. I edged my way towards the lamp.

The first blow connected to the side of my head. I stumbled against the closet door as muscular constrictor arms engulfed me from behind. The strong smell of cologne and stale breath greeted me. I struggled to escape, sensing a figure coming directly at me. My powerful kick landed solidly prompting a deep male grunt followed by a string of rapid angry Spanish. I planted my legs and pushed the man holding my arms backward into the mirror. The glass door rattled in its tracks but held. The man doubled the pressure on my arms in response to my attempt to twist him down to the floor. My body hung suspended and vulnerable as the second man landed punches to my gut and head. Several more of my kicks connected, but the second man kept coming. I tried one last time to free the first man's grip when another blow struck my head. Shooting stars zipped across my vision. A final punch launched me into a black hole.

CHAPTER 17

I regained consciousness in a fetal position on the floor facing a large window. My head and ribs exploded with pain, and the heavy metallic taste of blood lingered in my mouth. Light from a table lamp highlighted small blood stains on the beige carpet. Crusted blood covered my lips and chin.

"Arch Caldwell. Well, well. What a surprise to see an old friend."

The familiar voice belonged to a large handsome bald black man likely dressed in an expensive pin-striped suit and a gold diamond stud in his left ear. From the floor, I swiveled slowly around to peer at Junky sitting in a pea green corduroy armchair.

A hefty Hispanic man stood at Junky's right side, hovering over me. The man's hands showed signs of tenderness on the right knuckle from having worked me over. Junky never did the dirty work himself. The second man stood in the shadows just inside the hotel room door.

I sat up straight hoping to reduce the discomfort in my rib cage and head. I moved normally so as not to give present company the satisfaction of seeing the degree of pain they had inflicted. "Hi Junky. It's been a long-time. Thanks for the warm hospitality."

Junky let loose a deep resonating laugh that always reminded me of a baritone opera solo. He switched on a second table lamp to his right. "It's the least I can do for an old, armed acquaintance caught infiltrating one of my establishments. You should have known better, Arch."

"You're right, this isn't exactly the working over I had in mind."

"Next time don't use your personal credit card. I didn't think there could be another Arch Caldwell, the guy who tried to put me in jail." Junky gave me his best smile. His bleached teeth and prominent gold-capped incisor beamed, and made my head ache even more. "It's a good thing you weren't wearing a wire."

"Why would I be? I'm just a man pursuing a bit of fun while visiting his old haunts."

"You don't fool me, Arch. You sneak around pretending to be a businessman looking for a prostitute. I make it a habit of knowing my enemies. Tsk, tsk."

"Well, I didn't think I could just call and make an appointment to see you."

"No, you're probably right. Well, you have my full attention now, before Manny and Mako throw your ass in the ocean." He leaned forward, his hands resting on his knees, an inquisitive sparkle in his eyes.

I ignored the pain and pulled myself upright. "I came with what I hope is a lucrative business proposition for you."

He cocked his head in my direction and chuckled. "How intriguing. The least I can do is listen."

"I'm searching for a girl."

Junky nodded. "Aren't we all, Arch? Is that really why you shelled out the dough? Who is this girl?"

"Sarah Minor."

"Ah, a pretty one indeed. But if you need a girl, Arch, I can fix you up with someone more experienced, if you know what I mean."

"Sorry, I only have eyes for her."

"Is this what happens when the wife leaves?" Junky chuckled and glanced at his sidekick who didn't smile.

"She's somebody's daughter and I know you have her. I'll pay to take her off your hands." I got to my feet as the pain spread all over my body. I walked over to a desk chair, turned it around, and sat down gently. "You're still an asshole, Junky."

"Yeah, and I coulda put a bullet through your brain."

"Well, it would have been your loss."

"Since you retired from the force I was curious about why you decided to make a return appearance. What's so special about this girl?"

"That's my business. I'll give you fifteen grand for her."

Junky shook his head. "I'll need twenty. She's getting to be quite profitable."

"She's seventeen and a drug addict. I'm doing you a favor by taking her off your hands."

"You have a good point. How about we compromise at seventeen-five? You got the cash?"

"You'll have to call my banker, Benny McAllister."

His baritone laughter erupted. After his raucous outburst subsided, he gave me his classic grin. "You must be fucking kidding, Arch. Benny? He's an idiot."

"Didn't stop you from doing business with him all those years, now did it?"

His smirk disappeared. I'd hit the wrong nerve, putting my health in further jeopardy. "What's that fool got to do with this?"

I had to convince him to play ball. "Call him." Junky stared at me. "Go ahead and call him." I tried to convey the seriousness of my proposition while hiding my nervousness over having to depend on such a half-witted crook like my ex-partner. Frank Minor would have agreed to pay the money, but having Benny shell out his dirty dough seemed like a good idea. I hoped it didn't back-fire.

Junky pulled out his phone and hit a button. "Okay, I'll humor you, and then I'll have Mako chop up your body and spread the remains as chum for the sharks."

I found it ironic a man named Mako would turn me into shark bait.

Junky walked into the bedroom, his stern words barely audible as he whispered harsh warnings into the phone. Junky's voice suddenly boomed. "What were you thinking? You sent this asshole here?"

Junky listened for a long minute. I held my breath, which only aggravated my sore ribs. I searched the room for a weapon since my gun had disappeared. A lamp rested on one of the tables behind me. Given my physical condition, getting to it before Junky's boy put a bullet in me was unlikely. He stood large and intimidating; his Hispanic features made me conclude he was probably Manny. He stared into open space, his arms bulged in front of him, his left hand clasped over the right one. A gold chain hugged his huge neck, tattoos adorned his muscular forearms. Mako, the potential butcher, must have been the one stationed at the door. Junky employed some tough characters.

I had to hope my ex-partner accepted his role as my financial backer as the only way he could avoid jail. If he failed, things would get ugly. The odds were not in my favor to disarm Manny and get past Mako.

Junky returned to the room with the cell phone still glued to his ear. "I'll do it, but you're both dead if the cash isn't here by nine-thirty tomorrow morning." He ended the call. "Well, Arch, it looks like we have a deal. But if Benny fails you better both leave town."

"I'm not leaving without the girl."

"I admire your commitment." He paused. "How did you know about my boy at the restaurant?"

"I still have some connections at LAPD. Besides what do you care? You're making good money on the deal."

Junky rubbed his cleanly shaved chin. "Okay. Benny goes to the bank first thing in the morning and delivers the cash. You walk away with the girl." He strode over to a small wood desk, picked up the hotel stationary, and removed a pen from his inside suit jacket pocket. He wrote something on the paper and handed it to me. "Be at this address, nine-thirty tomorrow morning. On time."

I left the room grateful to be alive, and walked gingerly down to my car in the garage. I cursed myself for being naive and inexperienced. Andy would never have alerted Junky by paying his restaurant bill with his own credit card. Had I used cash and a fake name, I might have been driving away with the girl instead of retreating with a bruised body and ego.

I stopped at a Walgreen's to buy several brands of painkillers and a gigantic bottle of water. I parked around the corner from my hotel just in case Junky had any last minute regrets about our deal. He might prefer to take me out for good and forego the cash.

The street was quiet as midnight approached. I washed down some pain pills, reclined on my car seat, and waited for the pills to take effect. I woke an hour later and made the measured, painful walk to my hotel.

A hot bath provided only limited relief to my sore muscles. The stench of Mako's cologne persisted in my imagination. I checked the mirror—the hot water accentuated the cuts and bruises, and added a nice rainbow flush to my face.

I collapsed on the bed and thought about my first encounter with Junky during my first year on the police force. After graduating from the academy with high marks and ignorant enthusiasm, I was anxious to make a name for myself, an attribute encouraged by a father and brother who preceded me in the profession.

Could it have been only a year since I left the LAPD? It seemed such a long time ago. The bad memories combined with the painkillers coursing through my emotionally and physically ravaged body finally overcame the adrenalin of my encounter with Junky. The arrival of sleep relieved me from my disturbed reflections.

CHAPTER 18

The next morning my back and neck were frozen with tension and pain; my ribs hurt to inhale. Every muscle protested my slightest movement. The battle scars extended from my face down my chest to my waist.

After a hot shower and painkiller breakfast, I drove to the address Junky had given me. The large frosted numbers were stenciled on the glass doors of a plain brown brick apartment building.

The two men from the previous evening waited just inside the building's entrance. They escorted me to a second floor office where Junky sat hunched over a black laptop perched on a small folding table. The cheap furniture made it obvious Junky didn't spend much time here. "Wow Junky, I didn't know you could use a computer."

"Good morning, Arch. Don't be a wiseass. I take it you slept well."

"No thanks to your goons. I'll take my gun, if you don't mind."

"Sure." He reached into a desk drawer, removed my gun, and tossed it to me. The sudden movement to catch the weapon stunned my ribs. "Your buddy Benny made the payment. Mako here will take you to the girl." He nodded to a large black man sporting a dark well-trimmed afro and goatee.

An inaudible sigh caught in my throat.

"I'm a businessman, Arch. I do keep my word." Junky gave me a mischievous smile.

"That's comforting."

Junky studied the gun in my hand. The bullets were probably in the drawer. Otherwise, I might have shot all three of them right there, cleared Sarah and the girls out of the building, and torched it. How many more women were trapped in this building, locked in hopeless permanent servitude with no hope of career advancement? The safety was on. I stuck the gun into my waistband. My only desire was to get Sarah home. It would be a risk to step over the line without a loaded weapon.

I followed Mako to the door, but stopped and turned to the imposing figure whose huge stubby black fingers attempted to type on the diminutive keyboard. "I'll see you soon, Junky."

Junky flashed me the familiar warning stare. "Have a nice trip back to the Land of Chantment or whatever it's called. Nice doing business with you. I hope she's worth it."

I swallowed the temptation to ask about his relationship with Marconi to determine how their human trafficking enterprise functioned. My mind still worked the detective angle. Could I tie him to Andy's murder? I had studied Junky long enough to know it would have given him great pleasure to tell me, hoping to incite a violent reaction and give him the excuse to kill me, keep the money and the girl, and have my body pickled in the brine of the Pacific Ocean.

Andy would have walked out with the girl and not looked back. My plan had been clever enough, but the execution had been less than perfect. Retaliation would have to wait. I turned and slipped through the door.

Mako escorted me down a narrow dimly lit corridor with drab yellow walls. I noted the stairwell locations in case a quick exit was required. After several turns, we stopped and Mako pushed in a flimsy freshly-painted wood door. A double bed, small dresser, and a cheap wire lamp with a plastic shade on a nightstand filled most of the room. The drawn window drapes made it difficult to recognize the body lying on the bed. Mako turned on the lamp.

Sarah slept on her side in the fetal position, dressed in a sky blue terry cloth robe. Her breathing was shallow and raspy. Her mascara had splattered into random paint blotches around her eyes to resemble a Jackson Pollack painting. Despite the dark hair, her resemblance to Jesse was evident in the lamp's glow. The girl's youth had vanished, a result of too many drugs and too much time serving the sexual whim of strangers.

Mako shook her awake. She mumbled something about needing her rest. I bent down close to her ear. "Hi Sarah, my name is Arch. I need you to get up." She gazed at me with tormented blood-shot eyes, not the kind of eyes that should have belonged to an innocent teenaged girl.

"Leave me alone." She fixed me with a distrustful stare.

"My name is Arch Caldwell. Your father hired me to bring you home. Do you have any clothes?" She raised her head and glanced toward a small beige carry-all at the edge of the bed next to the nightstand. The oversized purse probably contained everything she owned.

I turned to Mako. "Can you grab that bag for me?" He turned unsuspectingly. I grabbed the gun from my waist and hit him as hard as I could on the back of the head. He collapsed, knocking into the nightstand. The lamp crashed onto his back. I hit him a second time and grabbed his gun, confirmed it was loaded, and put mine away. Mako deserved to wake up with a nice headache. Pretty sloppy of Junky to return my gun.

"What are you doing?" The activity seemed to get the girl's attention.

"Your mother wants you to come back home."

"My mother?"

"You remember your family back in New Mexico? Come on, I need you to get dressed." I shoved Mako's prone body aside to retrieve the bag, removed a blue denim dress, and handed it to her. I turned towards the door to give her some privacy.

We needed to get out before somebody discovered Mako. Call it revenge, or a message to Junky. I meant business. He wouldn't appreciate the gesture and might snuff me out like a cigarette under his shoe. But having Mako neutralized and being in possession of his loaded weapon evened the odds. Life isn't always fair, but sometimes the tables get turned the other way.

I checked to find Sarah had fallen back on the bed without even attempting to put on the dress. "I guess you're travelling in your bedroom attire. Come on." I shook her back awake.

She seemed to finally understand we were leaving. "Where we going?"

"For a ride in the desert. We need to leave."

Her eyes opened wide. "I need to tell Junky where I'm going."

"Junky doesn't control you anymore. I bought you, so you need to listen to me, Okay?"

"I guess."

I covered her with a thin blanket from the bed, gathered her up in my arms, and threw her slim body over my anguished shoulder. She couldn't have weighed more than 80 pounds. With her robe tied tightly around her, I scurried us through the empty hallway, down the nearest stairway, and out a door to my car around the corner.

She slumped against the passenger side door. "I'm tired."

"You can take a nap in the back seat." I opened the rear door and slid her onto the seat. Settled in behind the wheel, I fumbled with bullets from the glove compartment, trying to insert them into my gun. The ammo spilled onto the car floor. I dropped my gun on top of the bullets, placing Mako's loaded weapon on my lap. I accelerated, checking the rearview mirror, as the building fell out of view.

CHAPTER 19

I drove east on a main road. Pain swept over me. I struggled to keep my focus. The girl was safe with me, but we could be killed in a car crash if I didn't get some rest. I stopped at a large shopping center parking lot and searched my cell phone contacts to find the familiar number in the D section. He answered in a groggy voice.

"Hey DJ. It's Arch."

"Hey Buddy. I was sound asleep."

"Yeah, sorry. I need a favor." I tried to describe my location, but the surroundings were unfamiliar. Driving through the lot, I found a sign with the name of the shopping center. DJ recognized my location and described how to get back to the highway. I followed his directions for the 45-minute drive.

I pulled up in front of a fancy white brick apartment building on the edge of Beverly Hills. I left Sarah in the car and rang the doorbell. The intercom boomed with DJ's baritone voice. "That you Arch?"

"Yeah, DJ. Can you come down? I need help."

He arrived in the drab lobby, his bright red jumpsuit gave him the appearance of a chubby black Santa Claus. He had shaved his hair around his ears, the haircut enhanced his threatening image. Despite being the only black person in the building, DJ told me the owner and other residents loved having him there as a crime deterrent. Fortunately, they either didn't know or care he was gay.

We exchanged our traditional fist bump that sent shock waves through my body. I grimaced and my left hand shot out against a wall of mailboxes to catch my stumbling body.

DJ grabbed hold of my arm to steady me and peered at me closely. "Jesus, Arch. Your face looks like shit. What the hell happened?"

"I ran into an old enemy and his goons."

His face tensed. "Damn. That Junky dude do that to you? Where's the bastard? I'll get some friends and we'll go fuck him up."

"Not now DJ. I got a girl in the car. Can you bring her into the apartment?" We exited the lobby and walked down to the line of cars at the curb. I twitched instinctively as each car approached. Just being in the presence of the big man should have brought some calm. But I knew Junky's influence reached into many L.A. neighborhoods, the Hills being no exception.

He peered into the car. "Who's she?"

"My client's daughter. Junky had her. She's pretty messed up."

He reached into the back seat and lifted Sarah like a rag doll. She moaned as he carried her into the building. I picked up the bullets scattered around the passenger floor and stuck them and my gun into the glove compartment, keeping Mako's gun in my waistband. I staggered up the stairs to the apartment.

DJ laid Sarah down on the couch. "What's she doing, Arch?"

"Not sure. Maybe heroin or coke. It's going to get ugly later."

He shook his head. "You want some food?"

"Not now. I just need rest."

"And then what?"

"I'll take her to Phoenix. I know someone who might be able to help her, but it's going to be a hell of a ride once she starts to come down."

"Maybe, I should drive you. I can take some time off and fly back."

I knew my great friend's offer was sincere—his protection still a special gift long after our college partnership ended. As my career and life collapsed around me, I spent many nights on the couch in his previous apartment, a temporary sanctuary unknown to my enemies.

"Thanks, but I'll be able to make it if I can get just a few hours rest."

"If you're sure. I know how damn stubborn you are. You can crash in the spare bedroom and I'll keep an eye on the girl."

I stopped to take a piss and noticed the dabs of blood swirling around in the toilet bowl with my urine. From my post-football game experience, I figured my beating had resulted in minor internal damage.

The spare bedroom furnishings were as I remembered from his previous apartment placed with care in a bright comfortable room with gold walls reflecting the streaming sunlight from the window. A half-full crystal bowl of potpourri on the nightstand filled the room's air with a fresh scent. The pleasant ambiance brought the comfort DJ intended. Although I didn't think it would matter to my tired body, I closed the rose-colored drapes to dampen the light.

How can I describe DJ? He played left guard at UCLA and adopted me as his "little" white friend. We became inseparable. I came up with his nickname, because his facial features; freckled light brown skin, short-cropped reddish-brown hair, slight mustache, and warm smile reminded me of Dennis Johnson, a guard who had played for the Boston Celtics and Phoenix Suns, and later briefly became head coach for the Los Angeles Clippers. The similarity ended there—DJ's head and body more closely resembled a tank. Despite his 300 pounds, he could roll out from his tackle position on a sweep, lead the tailback to the hole, and plow right over the opposition's defensive player. Rather than call a number in the huddle, the quarterback referred to the pitch out as the 'DJ Slaughter'.

Born Albert Williams, the two-letter monogram became so familiar most people forgot his real name. His popularity expanded on campus—the University President used his initials, instead of his real name at the graduation ceremony bringing a big roar from our senior class. After graduation, he spent four years on the Raiders practice squad, hoping to eventually make the team and fulfill his dream of playing in the NFL. But despite his abilities, it never worked out and he now made good money working security at nearly every major sporting event in the L.A. area, including the Raiders home games. I had counted on his being home on a weekday morning, most likely after working a pro-basketball game the previous night.

I dialed Frank Minor's cell phone.

"Frank, I've got Sarah." I collapsed on the bed.

He gasped. "Oh my God. Is she okay? Where are you?"

"We're in L.A. She's pretty messed up from drugs. If it's all right with you I'm going to take her to a clinic in Scottsdale run by a friend

113

of mine. He'll be able to help her. She's underage, so you'll need to grant me permission."

"Of course, Arch. Do what you think is best for her."

"You'll need to get to the clinic or call them if you want to leave her there, or you can pick her up and take her somewhere else. I'll be there in about six hours."

"I can get a flight later today and be there by evening."

"I'll let them know you're arriving tonight. They can hold her until you get to the clinic tomorrow morning and decide what you want to do. The clinic has a great reputation." I gave him the contact information. He thanked me several times before we disconnected.

I called the clinic but couldn't reach my old friend from high school, Sal Cangeloni. My call was transferred from a receptionist through an automated message system. Sal served as the head administrator. The Cangelonis had owned a chain of Italian restaurants in Phoenix, and Sal could have entered the family business and made a fortune after graduating from University of Arizona. But after his older sister died of a drug overdose, he opted for medical school, eventually opening his own clinic. When his voicemail prompted me, I left Sal a message letting him know I was bringing in a patient and it might be near closing time.

I lay down on the queen bed and stared at the white ceiling. As the pain subsided, my bruised body drifted into therapeutic sleep.

• • •

DJ's booming voice in the other room roused me out of my nap. According to the clock radio, I had been asleep for just over an hour. The pain returned as I sat up and my feet hit the floor.

I walked into the kitchen where DJ fed Sarah small mouthfuls of split pea soup. She seemed to be enjoying the food, although her eating before the drugs wore off during a long trip couldn't be a good thing. The Linda Blair vomiting scene from The Exorcist flashed across my mind, bringing on a touch of my own nausea.

DJ smiled. "I made some soup. Have a seat." He went into the kitchen and returned with a large bowl and a warm piece of bread. "Did you call her family?"

I nodded. "Her father's going to meet us in Phoenix."

He placed the food in front of me. "It's sourdough. I made it last night."

I dipped the bread into the soup and the taste exploded in my mouth. "You need to open a café."

"Yeah, how many years we be saying that, my man?"

"Too many. But when I strike it rich…"

It was a conversation often repeated between us, but this time I couldn't keep it going. The idea that we would save enough money to open a restaurant had been a fantasy dependent upon my success in the law enforcement field and DJ's signing a lucrative contract to play in the pros. Neither scenario had panned out, so the dream had yielded to the real world—just trying to make ends meet. He seemed to be doing a better job at it than me.

He laughed and shrugged. "I'm doing fine, Arch. I've accepted my fate. I even met a nice guy. We've gone out a couple of times so we'll see. And what about Jo and Jo?"

The names were how he referred to my wife and daughter. "I think they're in Vegas. I haven't been in touch. Josie's birthday is coming up."

He grabbed my hand. "You gotta go, man. You gotta go see that little girl of yours." His eyes lit up and his voice trembled. I knew he loved me like a brother.

"I'm planning on it."

He nodded and smiled. But he knew of the anguish still haunting me from my L.A. days. "You need to settle your score with Junky or just let it go."

"I thought I had let it go, but then this case came along. It's fate dragging me back in. Now I don't know what to feel."

DJ crossed his arms over his massive chest. "Next time, you come get me, you hear?"

"He's a bad dude, DJ. I don't want to get you involved in my fight. I haven't had much success battling this guy."

"The problem Arch is you've got a heart and Junky don't."

"Yeah, but mine feels pretty busted up right now, and not just emotionally."

"I hear you, man. You're a lot tougher than you let on. I know this for a fact. So, don't bullshit me. You'll recover and then decide what you want to do about Junky. You consult with me first. I got acquaintances."

I smiled, although it hurt. "I know you do. If I were going to war, I know who I'd want by my side."

"It will be war and I'll be there for you if you want."

"No, I was thinking of Randle." DJ rocked with laughter. Randle, had been a teammate of ours who played defensive end. Every week he had some ailment he claimed was serious enough to keep him out of the next game. We waged bets behind his back, trying to predict what would develop as the next week's ailment.

DJ was still snickering. "That pussy. Well, I'm glad you still got your sense of humor. Hold on." He left the room while I finished the soup.

When DJ returned, he handed me a prescription bottle. "Courtesy of the Raidas." He pronounced the team name imitating the voice of a former sportscaster named Howard Cosell. "They're strong and will perk you right up. I'll also brew you up some coffee to take. Sorry, but those are my last pills. I ain't got those same connections no more. If you can wait, I'll scrounge some up from my other sports friends."

"No, it's okay. These will get me to Phoenix." At that point, an overdose of pain meds would have seemed like relief, but getting Sarah to Phoenix was my next goal. I had to take one excruciating step at a time.

He equipped me with a gigantic thermos of strong black coffee, and helped Sarah into the backseat of the car. We wrapped her in the blankets, and DJ added a purple plastic pail. "You never know."

I laughed. "You think she'll hit it?"

"There's always a chance."

I got in and started the engine. DJ held the door open with a frown. He gave me a soft fist bump. "You be careful, Arch. Call if you need anything."

"You got it." Several pills slid down my throat with a gulp of hot coffee. He shut the door and I headed for the I-10.

CHAPTER 20

I cruised along the I-10 towards Phoenix, oblivious to the picturesque desert landscape, until the pain and fatigue double-teamed me. A truck stop appeared like an oasis just shy of the Arizona border. Sarah had been sick and the vehicle smelled of vomit. Her moaning suggested she was having a bad detox. After parking on the perimeter of the truck stop, I got out to check on her. Rolled up in her bathrobe and thin blanket, she quivered with chills and fever—her forehead burned to my touch.

I locked the car and tossed the filthy plastic floor mat with the congealed vomit into a garbage can. Sarah had missed the pail.

A convenience store and attached restaurant lay just beyond the nearby fuel pumps. I glanced back to make sure Sarah didn't get out and go for a zombie stroll through the parking lot. It wouldn't look good to be seen dragging a drugged-up teenager in her robe back to the car.

A battered swollen face, bruised cheeks and puffy eyes stared back at me in the service station restroom mirror. The cold water and anti-bacterial soap from a wall dispenser stung as I washed the cuts around my nose and mouth. It woke me up.

The small store featured the usual tourist paraphernalia, along with rows of snacks and a corner filled with Native American gift selections. I purchased a cotton blanket, several bottles of water, and two cups of coffee from a square machine.

I returned to the car with a plastic bag containing the blanket and the water, and balancing the coffees on a cardboard carrier. The caffeine would do both of us some good. I encouraged Sarah to sit up. Her eyes were half-shut and she sat with her arms wrapped tightly around her as if bound in a straightjacket.

"I've got some coffee. It will help you feel a little better."

Sarah nodded, although her eyes fluttered on the verge of closing.

"But first I want you to drink some water because you're probably dehydrated. Ready?" I opened the bottle and tipped it to her lips, but the liquid dribbled down her chin onto her robe. "Come on Sarah, you need to drink this and then I'll give you the coffee."

Her eyes opened and she snarled at me. "Screw you."

"Yeah, well I'm not crazy about you either. You threw up all over my car. Maybe one day you'll thank me for this."

Her indignant look softened and she closed her eyes.

"I'm trying to help you. Your family asked me to find you."

She opened her eyes. I motioned with the bottle and this time she drank, taking small baby sips that grew to substantial swallows. Her throat must have been raw from vomiting. She finished half the water; her thirst now quenched after riding with the sun beating down on her through the rear window.

She nodded before handing back the half-empty bottle. I placed it in the backseat cup holder and handed her the coffee. "Here, try some of this, the caffeine will give you a little jolt and help the withdrawal. Careful, it's a bit hot. She placed both hands around the coffee cup.

It's going to be a rough couple of hours until we get to Phoenix where I can get you some real help." She shivered despite the heat, so I wrapped both blankets around her. "You can put the cup in the holder here if you don't want to drink it now."

I filled the tank with gas, eased into the driver's seat, and started the car. The AC blowers had been set to blast the cold air to keep me awake. I reduced the flow, directing it at me instead of to the rear of the vehicle, where Sarah sat wrapped in the blanket like a vertical burrito. I popped the last painkiller and washed it down with the water. Sarah's blank face stared back at me in the rearview mirror, a few tears trickled down her cheek. She retrieved the coffee and slowly sipped the warm liquid.

"Next stop Phoenix. Well technically, Scottsdale."

She nodded as I took a couple of sips of the bitter coffee, hoping the caffeine would help keep me awake for the next few hours.

• • •

We arrived in the Phoenix area just after peak rush hour, but the traffic slowed to a crawl before reaching the 101 turnoff to Scottsdale. A half-hour later, I pulled up to the clinic at sunset, relieved to see lights on. I stumbled up a long cement ramp flanked by metal guardrails to find the doors unlocked.

The Waldron Drug Treatment Center resembled a small cruise ship thanks to the porthole windows lining multiple floors of the white building. The design must have allowed some light into the building, but the windows were small enough to reduce exposure to the sun and dissuade patients from thinking they could jump out the window.

Sarah had returned to her fetal position and hardly responded when I returned to the car. The strong smell of urine blindsided me after unraveling her from the blanket. I placed her over my shoulder and shuffled up the ramp through the doors. The receptionist seemed unconcerned about the human bundle slumped down my back.

"I'm looking for Sal."

The middle-aged woman dressed in a formal gray suit finally glanced up from her paperwork. "Well sir, I'm not sure where he is right now. We're about to close." She started to swivel her chair in the opposite direction.

"Just page him and tell him Arch Caldwell is here."

With the mention of my name she nodded and turned to her phone. "Sorry, yes we were expecting you." Please have a seat while I page him."

Despite Sarah's frail figure, her weight tugged on my sore ribs. I plopped her down in one of several guest chairs along the reception area wall. She fell sideways and moaned. "Where are we?"

"We're at a friend's place. Someone who will take good care of you."

Fatigue overcame me and I nearly dozed off in one of the adjacent seats until I heard, "Arch, is that you?"

I gingerly stood up and received a solid handshake from the short and stocky Sal. He had gained a few pounds and his thick coal-black hair had receded in the area above his temples. He studied me and grimaced. "Man, are you Okay? You look like hell."

"Yeah, I got into a little altercation in L.A."

"I thought you got out of there?"

"I did. But I had to retrieve the girl and got some resistance from her friendly caregivers. You got my message?"

"Yes, I've been waiting for you." He walked over to where Sarah slouched in the chair.

"I've got the paperwork started. Any idea which drugs she's been taking?" He said it casually, like an everyday experience.

"Possibly heroin or cocaine, or maybe both. She's a real mess. Can you help?"

"Of course. How old is she?" He pulled out a small flashlight from his white lab coat that covered his dark cotton business suit. He gently moved Sarah upright to peer into her eyes.

"She's seventeen, going on thirty. Her name is Sarah Minor. Her dad's got enough money to pay for the treatment costs."

He nodded and stroked his short well-trimmed goatee. "I know. I spoke with him this afternoon. He seemed convinced of our qualifications and gave us permission to keep her here." He turned to the receptionist. "Margaret, please ask Jorge and Michael to come to the reception area."

He turned back to me. "By the way, he was trying to call you on your cell phone."

I had forgotten about my phone left in the car. "I was so intent on getting here, I didn't check my messages."

"He's on his way from Albuquerque. He should be in Phoenix tonight and here first thing tomorrow morning. He wanted me to tell you to go home rather than wait here for him to arrive."

The two orderlies arrived and lifted Sarah. She tried to struggle, but she gave up and her body went limp. They placed her in a wheelchair.

I walked back over to Sarah. "Sarah, I'm leaving you here. You'll be in good hands with Dr. Sal." As Sal conversed with the assistants, I returned to my car to retrieve my cell phone. Three voicemail messages awaited me from Sarah's family. Barb and Frank called to thank me. Frank reiterated his preference for me to go home. Jesse also voiced her appreciation and added a request for me to call her when I got back because she wanted to see me. The evocative tone of her voice made me temporarily forget my fatigue.

Sal greeted me just inside the clinic door. "Arch, let me get a nurse to clean you up and dress those bruises."

"No, I'll be fine. I want to make it to Albuquerque tonight."

"Are you sure you can drive?"

"I need to get home. I really appreciate this, Sal. I owe you one."

Sal reached over and gripped my arm. "You need rest, but I know better than to try and talk you out of anything."

I focused on Sal's face. "She'll be okay?"

He gave me an encouraging nod, shook my hand, and followed his two white-coated staff toward a glass door to the right of the reception desk.

Sal turned just before entering the doorway. "Call me in a couple of days."

I thanked Sal again, walked over to the reception desk, and grabbed a couple of business cards. The receptionist had left for the evening. I considered spending the night at my parent's house, but my appearance would only invite questions and criticism from my mother, and continued ambivalence from my father. My phone rang as I exited the clinic doors. I didn't recognize the number.

"Hello."

"Arch, this is Gordy."

"Hey Gordy. I didn't expect to hear from you so soon."

"I'm sure. Just wanted to let you know I heard some cops at happy hour. Your name came up at Outlaws and not in a friendly way, if you know what I mean. Seems your return is no longer secret."

"I'm not surprised."

"Well, you better watch your back or get out of town."

"I'm on my way home, but I appreciate the warning, Gordy. You stay safe there."

"Don't worry about me. Drive carefully." He hung up.

My exhaustion disappeared with the news. My return to L.A. had stirred up some anxiety. I edged down the ramp to my car, slid behind the wheel, and took one long deep breath, dreading the six-hour drive to Albuquerque.

CHAPTER 21

My body had already raised the white flag of surrender by the time I reached Albuquerque just after 1:30 a.m. A short nap in a New Mexico rest area had provided just enough of a break to keep me going. I headed straight to the office, which was closer to the highway than my apartment.

I pulled up outside my building and left the windows open, hoping the cool air would dissipate the odor inside. Anyone desperate enough to steal a car with such a foul smell would be doing me a favor.

My ribs were on fire. I hobbled up the steps to my second story office, holding on to the railing, hoisting myself up like someone yanking on a pulley. Before opening my office door, I visited the restroom at the end of the hall and checked myself in the mirror above the sink. The bruises beside and below my right eye had turned a deep shade of purple. My face had swelled even more. Dried blood speckled my lips and the front of my shirt.

I washed my face, returned to the office, and pulled out a bottle of Advil from my top desk drawer. My stomach growled with hunger, but I was too tired to eat, even if there had been any food in the office.

Thanks to the dearth of cases, the half-empty bottom file drawer contained plenty of room in the back for a large bottle of Jack Daniels. I washed down several pills with a good swig of whiskey. Sorry Josie, this is a medical emergency.

The effects of fatigue and booze flooded over me. I fell asleep with my legs on the desk only to jerk awake several times, reimagining the punches landing to my body by Junky's henchmen. I finally fell asleep until I heard a female voice, "Oh my God. What happened to you?"

Through puffy eyes, I saw Jesse standing in an angelic pose at the doorway to my office. Her beauty almost relieved the pain. Almost.

She came over and touched my bruised face. "Thank you for what you did."

I nodded but not forcefully enough to knock her hand off my cheek. "I'm glad I found her."

"You look like you got into a fight on the playground."

"No, more like in a house of ill repute." My sleeping legs buzzed as they landed on the floor.

"Did you refuse to pay? Don't move. I'll be right back."

"Don't worry. I'm not moving." She grabbed a "Money" magazine off my desk and disappeared. A few minutes later, she returned with a black case she placed on top of the desk.

"You were just dying to read that issue?"

"I used it to prop the door open. I figured the security guy locked it."

"Good thinking. Wait, what are you doing here?" I tried to de-emphasize any complaint in my voice.

"I drove down after my father called to tell me you had found Sarah. We had an early dinner and I dropped him off at the airport. I got your message that you were driving back tonight. I went to a sushi bar around the corner and had a few glasses of wine. So, rather than drive back to Santa Fe, I checked your apartment. You weren't there so I came by your office. I drove past and saw your car parked in front and your light on." The thought of her insistence at finding me warmed my neglected heart, one of my muscles not currently in agony.

"How did you get in the building?" My brain had started to recover just from the sight of her.

"I had to sweet-talk a security guard who was making his rounds outside. I told him I was your wife. You were working late and I wanted to surprise you. He confirmed your light was on in your office and let me in."

"You must have made his night. Imagine falling for the 'I'm his wife' routine. Remind me to have him fired first thing in the morning."

"Is there a bathroom up here?"

I waved my hand. "Down the hall to your right. Here, you'll need the key." She grabbed it and headed out the office door with her case.

She returned with some damp cloths. "Can you lie down over here on the couch?"

I had forgotten about the couch. It didn't quite hold my six-foot frame, although even with my legs looped over the arm, it was more comfortable than my contorted position behind the desk.

Her hands touched my side. I flinched. She lifted my shirt and saw bruises painted over my rib cage. She sighed. "They could be broken."

"No, just bruised."

"How can you be so sure?"

"I played wide-receiver at UCLA. Believe me, I know what bruised ribs feel like."

"I should take you to the emergency room. You could have internal bleeding." She let my shirt drop and turned to her black case.

"No, really I'll be fine. And besides I feel like I'm in good hands, right here."

"Typical stubborn man." She opened her case filled to the brim with an assortment of bottles, bandages, and ointments.

"You carry that case with you all the time?"

"Yes, I keep it in my car. You just never know. Let's clean you up." She sat down on the edge of the couch and leaned over me. Her subtle musky perfume and hint of alcohol on her breath washed over me like an aphrodisiac. She used the cloths to wash my face and then reached into her case and extracted a white tube. "This will help the healing." She gently applied the greasy lubricant—her hands caressed my skin.

"Did you take anything for the pain?"

"I took a couple of Advil." I peeked at my watch. "About an hour ago."

Jesse wiped her hands on the cloth, pulled out a bottle, and handed me a pill. "Take this. It will really knock out the pain."

"Don't say those words."

"Which ones?"

"Knock out. I feel like I just went one round with Ali."

"You made it through the first round?"

"Barely."

I took the pill and looked at the bottle of Jack still sitting on the desk. She frowned. "I'll get you some water. These are prescription painkillers. It's better not to take them with any booze." She grabbed a coffee cup from my desktop, and filled it in the bathroom down the hall. I washed down the pill and started to hand her back the cup. "No, you better drink the whole thing."

Jesse discovered the motel-sized refrigerator and freezer in the office corner and returned with several pieces of white cloth filled with ice cubes. She touched the cold cloths, like bookends, to the bruised spots on the each side of my head. A tear had formed at the corner of her right eye and her voice quivered. "Where was she?"

"Your father didn't tell you?"

"No, remember, need-to-know only."

I nodded. "Junky had her at one of his establishments."

"A whorehouse?"

"Yes, I'm sorry." I pulled out the business card from my dress shirt pocket and handed it to her. "But she's in good hands now. This guy Sal is a friend of mine. Sarah's really messed up. She's going to need some serious professional care."

Jesse glanced at the card and then at me. I couldn't quite interpret the expression. Appreciation? Fondness? Exasperation?

"And this happened while you were retrieving my sister? This Junky, he did this?" She held the ice to the bulls-eye on my bruised cheek just below my right eye.

"Not him personally. He has others dish out punishment on his behalf. But, hey, you should see the other guys."

"I'll go see her tomorrow." She kissed me on the forehead and continued to touch the side of my head with the ice. Shivers erupted through my body cavity, but not from the ice.

I grabbed her hand. "Jesse, I don't think you want to see her just yet. Give her a few days to recover. She'll have to go through a lot."

She frowned. "I can't even imagine what she's been through. What are you going to do now?"

"I need to go home, take a shower, and get some sleep." I worried about how badly I smelled.

I started to get up from the couch, but rose too quickly. Pain streaked through my diaphragm and drove me back down.

Jesse grabbed for me. "Can you drive anymore?"

"I could probably make it to my house, but I'd appreciate a lift home. My car is in rough shape." Jesse put an arm around me and helped me slowly to my feet. She reached out and grabbed her case with her free hand.

"I'm glad you're tall." I put my hand on her shoulder as we edged down the stairs.

"I've had a few boyfriends who were intimidated by my height."

"The short boyfriends?"

"No, even a few of the tall ones."

"Sounds like you've dated a lot of guys."

She smiled. "Not many, really. I'm pretty picky."

"Me too." I tried to sound convincing, despite being dismayed that she apparently had considerably more dating experience.

"Your height must have come in handy playing volleyball. You were good?" I meant it as a compliment, but the pills and booze made it sound more like a question.

"I was competitive. I mostly played beach volleyball while attending San Diego State. It was fun."

"I would have paid to see that." A vision of Jesse playing volleyball in a bikini on a sunny California beach almost made me lose my footing.

It took us about 10 minutes to get down the stairs. Luckily, her car sat right behind mine near the door.

She drove me home and got me into my apartment. My brain danced in quicksand. I tried to concentrate while she talked about her sister. I wanted to hear every word even if the memory faded by morning.

She helped me to my bedroom and slipped off my shoes as I spiraled into a zombie state on the bed. So much for the shower. It would have to wait until after a few hours rest.

I heard her talking to me through a fog as she reached over and put a small bottle on my nightstand. "Take one of these capsules, three times a day."

"What are those?" I mumbled.

"A natural concoction of about eleven herbs and spices to help you recover."

I managed a retort about turning into a piece of Kentucky fried chicken before fading into a half-dream world. I heard her voice but couldn't make out the words. She might have inquired as to whether or not I might be finger lickin' good, but it could have been a hopeful hallucination.

I opened my eyes briefly and saw her standing over me. She said something about going back to her father's house to spend the night. I murmured something about her being a beautiful angel before I fell into a deep sleep.

CHAPTER 22

Three days later, I crawled out of bed after nearly 10 hours of sleep grateful some of my discomfort had finally subsided. I popped the last painkiller and another herbal concoction capsule from the white unmarked bottle Jesse had left on my bedside table. Having my own attractive health provider came with a number of intangible benefits. She had called every day since my return from L.A. to inquire about my health. Her concern quickened my recovery.

My scruffy image stared back at me in the bathroom mirror. I shaved for the first time since returning from L.A. My face had been too sore to bother removing the itchy coarse stubble covering my jaws and neck. The swelling had receded, the cuts and bruises no longer visible. Although my ribs still hurt, with a clean face I began to resemble my old charming self.

My appetite had returned. I made a breakfast of eggs, toast, and a large cup of coffee took the edge off the pain medication. I added a bowl of yogurt and fresh strawberries to my Breakfast of Champions.

Andy's funeral was scheduled for 10:00. I dressed in an old dark suit from the closet and headed out the door. My car had been returned the day before, following a thorough detailing and fumigation. Frank Minor sounded understanding regarding the cost, but he hadn't yet received the bill. An overpowering bouquet of cinnamon and spice deodorizer hit me when I opened the car door. Despite the chilled air, I rolled the window down.

I called Detective Burns for news on Andy's murder investigation. His family would expect me to provide an update. Burns didn't have much to add to what I already knew.

The funeral occurred on a perfect fall day without a cloud in the crystal blue New Mexico sky, the kind of day Andy always boasted about when we were in California. He claimed the California sky became dulled by too much particulate matter, and the mountains slumped as if they wanted to be somewhere else. He bragged about what he referred to as the manly rugged slopes of the Sandia Mountains hovering menacingly over the Rio Grande valley.

I entered Sunset Memorial Park, a green oasis surrounded by industrial and office complexes in the shadow of I-25. Towering pines, spruce and elms dominated the landscape of luminous grass. I drove down a black top road that split the velvet Verde like an extended rip in a pool table cover. Clumps of red, yellow, and white flowers in small vases dotted the lawn, memorials to friends and loved ones. The road names of Tulip, Rose, Canna, and Daisy added to the botanical atmosphere.

A group of mourners gathered on a hilltop near the back of the cemetery. I parked as close as possible along a section of road lined with tall cedars. Despite the view, the sounds of traffic on the nearby interstate and a powerful antiquated riding lawnmower spoiled the tranquility. I climbed from the car, struggled up the hill, and picked my way carefully to avoid the dual rows of head stones lined up like dominoes. My legs, inactive for too long, longed for me to break into a sprint, but the climb to the crest of the hill brought back the ache in my ribs.

Andy came from a huge family. A crowd of relatives and friends had already formed a ring around the casket hovering above the rectangular void. I positioned myself at the perimeter of the tent. Thanks to my height, I could see Andy's family members seated on white folding chairs at the edge of the hole.

The wind picked up as the service started. A whiff of diesel from the lawnmower drifted over as leaves in the overhanging trees began to rustle. The cacophony of sounds drowned out most of the priest's prayers. That was fine with me since I had already detached myself from the words with memories of Andy. I mentally prepared an optimistic summary of the murder investigation in response to the anticipated inquiries from Andy's father.

Following the service, Sarah's mother, Barbara came over and hugged me. "Our family will always be grateful for what you did. I'm so sorry about Andy." I followed her gaze to our right and saw Andy's dad making a beeline straight for us. Barb started down the hill before Mr. Lujan arrived to grasp my outstretched hand. I offered my condolences.

He held on to my hand with a solid grip and guided me conspiratorially over to the shade of a large elm tree, away from the departing crowd. "My son was fond of you, Arch. He said you were a good detective."

I could see the redness and swelling in his eyes—parents shouldn't outlive their offspring. "Not nearly as good as he was. He was a good friend and mentor, Mr. Lujan." I addressed him formally; a courtesy extended not just to a friend's father, but to a man, who like many others with the same last name had served in state politics for years. Having lost his wife a few years before, Pete Lujan now spent his retirement gardening or fly fishing in one of the northern mountain's famous streams. Andy had dragged me along occasionally when he met his father for dinner.

Gripping my shoulder, he peered into my eyes—his intensity reverberated in my soul. "When my wife died, I didn't think I could survive, but I consoled myself knowing my kids would help me make it through. Despite Andy's becoming a cop, I never expected to outlive my son."

I nodded and waited.

"Do the police have any leads?"

"Not at this time, Mr. Lujan, but the investigation has just started."

"Arch, you find out who killed my son." His grip tightened on my shoulder.

"I will, Mr. Lujan. I've got a suspect. He's a man Andy knew who may have had a motive to kill him. I'm trying to connect the dots and build a case."

"Thanks Arch. That makes me feel better." He released his grip and slowly limped away, his shoulders hunched as if he would topple over with the slightest push. He stopped and turned back to me. "I still know a lot of people in the government. You let me know if you need any help, Arch."

"You have my word, Mr. Lujan."

I saw Andy's older sister, Beverly, and headed her way. A schoolteacher in the Albuquerque public schools, she represented all the good embodied in human beings. Andy had admired her more than anyone else in the world because of her dignity, intelligence, and humility. With her dark hair, cut short around a plain face, she teetered on the verge of being pretty, but age had begun to tip the scales.

Several funeral guests lingered around to pay their respects. Finally, Beverly saw me and I greeted her with a genuine hug despite the acute discomfort in my ribs. She pulled away. The tears brimmed in her eyes, the same emerald color as Andy's, but bolder. The mascara threatened to dribble down her cheek.

"I'm so sorry Bev."

"Thank you, Arch."

"You know if there is anything I can do..."

She forced a grin of thanks. "The police don't have a clue who killed him."

"It's still early in the investigation."

She held my arm. "Will you help?"

"I promised your dad I would. I'm already working on it."

She nodded and stared down to the row of cars. Following her gaze, I saw Barbara Carson's Camry pulling away from the curb. Bev had a hateful look in her eyes. "I'm certain his death had something to do with her family."

"Maybe. I'll find out for sure."

She gave me a pat on my arm and turned to locate her husband and children only to encounter another line of funeral attendees waiting patiently to mumble words of consolation.

I wanted to catch Barbara, but the BMW already headed toward the cemetery exit. The walk back down the hill loosened my muscles and eased some of the soreness. The pain pills and caffeine from that morning's coffee engaged in a tug of war to keep me in limbo between tired and alert. By the time I reached my car, the pills won the battle and forced me back to my apartment for a nap.

"It's still early in the investigation."

She held my arm. "Will you help?"

"I promised your dad I would. I'm already working on it."

She nodded and stared down to the row of cars. Following her gaze, I saw Barbara Carson's Camry pulling away from the curb. Bev had a hateful look in her eyes. "I'm certain his death had something to do with her family."

"Maybe. I'll find out for sure."

She gave me a pat on my arm and turned to locate her husband and children only to encounter another line of funeral attendees waiting patiently to mumble words of consolation.

I wanted to catch Barbara, but the BMW already headed toward the cemetery exit. The walk back down the hill loosened my muscles and eased some of the soreness. The pain pills and caffeine from that morning's coffee engaged in a tug of war to keep me in limbo between tired and alert. By the time I reached my car, the pills won the battle and forced me back to my apartment for a nap.

CHAPTER 23

My cell phone's jingle woke me from a chemically-induced slumber.

"Hi, it's me, Jesse." Just hearing her voice cleared away the mist from my brain.

"Hi Jesse. I was sleeping."

"Oh, I'm sorry. You need your rest."

"It's fine. I've been sleeping for hours. Those pills you gave me were potent." I sat up at full attention.

"Are they helping with the pain?"

"As much as possible. I'm glad you called."

"I wanted to go see my sister, but I can't drive for long periods alone. You know, because of my cataplexy. I take the medication, but there's always a chance of a seizure. Since I'm off tomorrow and Monday I was wondering if maybe you could drive with me. We can take my car."

"Mine smells like a spice factory, so we don't have a choice."

"What?"

"Never mind."

"I'll pay for the gas and everything. We can stay over and get a hotel room. I'll pay."

I enthusiastically agreed. The thought of spending time with her sounded better than lying on the couch watching football with a beer and a heating pad.

• • •

She picked me up at 6:00 am the next morning and we headed west on I-40 as the sun rose behind us. It was a beautiful windless fall morning. She looked radiant. I tried not to stare. "So, what happens if you get an attack while you're driving?"

"You ever experienced road rage?"

"Not me personally."

"Well, this is the ultimate road rage. I start cursing and whatever is loose and available becomes a projectile."

"Sounds very attractive." I tried to sound facetious, but the vision of this beauty on a violent rampage was intriguing.

"Yes, if you're into that kind of thing." She laughed, as if reading my mind. "It's really not very pleasant. But it hasn't happened in a long time."

"Well let me know if you feel an urge coming on."

"The medication seems to be working, lucky for you." She squirmed in her seat.

She talked non-stop about her relationship with Sarah and her parent's divorce. "It was not an amicable split. I was old enough to understand or maybe accept it. As a young teenager, Sarah took it harder and never seemed to recover."

"It must have been difficult even for you."

"I had been through so much. My condition has proved to be a life-long challenge. I was only eight when they determined the cause of my irrationality. I fell into a deep depression, which meant years of anti-depressants in addition to the medication they prescribed to control my erratic behavior. I thought my life was over."

"But you got through it. What helped you turn the corner?"

"Sports. Thanks to my height, both the high school basketball and volleyball coaches were heavily recruiting me to tryout. Volleyball stuck. My concentration improved and so did my grades. I got a scholarship to play college volleyball and was an alternate for the Olympic team."

"Very impressive." I turned to study her pleasant profile.

"I wasn't quite good enough. There were too many better women athletes ahead of me."

"How did you get into nursing?"

"With all the medical problems I had, it just seemed natural, although the commitment to it didn't occur until my junior year in college. Up to that point, I didn't know what to declare as a major. I graduated with a BS in nursing and then continued on to get certified as a surgical assistant before moving back to New Mexico."

"So, you're right in there during surgery?"

"Yes, I'm also registered for critical care work, so I can follow up with the patients who need it." She glanced at the rearview mirror and blind spot before passing a slow-moving U-Haul.

"That must be challenging."

"It's also rewarding when you see patients recover."

"Sounds like you will be a great help to your sister."

Jesse got quiet for about five minutes with the mention of Sarah. "You're from Phoenix, right?"

"Born and raised. Lived there until college."

"Do you still have family there?"

"My parents and brother, and his family. My dad is a retired Phoenix cop. My mom still works part-time at a local dry cleaner. My brother, Bart, is an Arizona state trooper."

"Wow, law enforcement really does run in your blood. Your mom is probably the only sane one in your family." A smile flashed across her face.

"You may be on to something there."

"Maybe your brother will pull us over. What a surprise that would be…" She glanced over with raised eyebrows.

"If you don't slow down, there's a good possibility."

Jesse seemed content from the moment we hit the interstate. I got the impression that prolonged highway driving was not something she attempted very frequently due to her medical condition. The car occasionally lunged forward as she pressed firmly on the accelerator, an unconscious reaction that occurred as she engaged in animated discussion. Just as suddenly, she would let off the gas pedal when she glanced at the rising speedometer.

With a reluctant sigh, she suddenly acknowledged this phenomenon. "Sorry, I rarely get to cut loose on the interstate." She began fiddling with a knob on the steering wheel. "I do have cruise control."

I raised my hands in mock resignation. "Hey, knock yourself out."

"It's amazing how the law enforcement profession seems to be inherited. Did you always want to be a cop?"

"No, I wanted to play for the Oakland Raiders, but when I didn't get drafted it was about the only option left with a Physical Education degree from UCLA."

"Is your family close?"

"I haven't spoken to my father or brother in almost a year."

Her mouth dropped. "Because of the indictment? But you told me you were acquitted."

"Yes, but they assumed I was guilty. I didn't take any money or physically protect the criminals, but I condoned the activity by not turning in the crooked cops. I'm just as guilty, if for nothing else then by association."

"But, they're family. They should stick by you no matter what. Look at my dysfunctional family, and yet we're there for each other."

"That's nice." I meant it. "My mother calls me occasionally when my dad isn't around. You can't cancel a mother's love no matter how badly you've acted."

Jesse pouted. "She has to sneak around just to call you?" She shook her head.

We drove in silence for a while before she asked, "So how did you meet your wife?"

I told her about meeting Joanne during the autopsy of a prostitute's body at the morgue. Benny and I were assigned the case. We arrived to inspect the corpse and encountered the Chief Coroner and his assistant named Joanne Summerall. The naked somewhat preserved victim rested on a gurney. Purple bruises marked the body and what remained of her head resembled a folded rubber Halloween mask. Having just concluded their autopsy, the coroner provided his summary that the victim had been shot at close range in the back of the head, explained by the exit wound in the anterior brain section. Fluids spilled out onto the gurney when the body was turned over, prompting the queasy feeling in my gut already building from viewing the mangled corpse and breathing the nauseous smell of embalming chemicals.

As a distraction, I glanced at Joanne in her white medical burka; the long white lab coat, and matching gloves, surgical cap, and facial mask. She returned my gaze, her mouth hidden while her eyes smiled above the mask. I thought about firing back my best smile, but it seemed inappropriate to flirt while a battered body lay in front of us.

I didn't speak to Joanne until a second prostitute witness turned up dead a few months later. The same cause of death. Benny declined a second trip to the morgue, an experience I would have avoided except for my commitment to solve the case. I also wanted another opportunity to see Joanne. This time she conducted the autopsy solo. She appeared competent and ambitious, a necessary combination for a woman climbing the medical examiner's hierarchy.

"I acted more composed on the second trip to the morgue, primarily to impress Joanne. She disagreed with the Chief's conclusion that the bruises on the first woman occurred during a fall after the fatal shot. Joanne's examination concluded the second woman had been beaten and tortured before murder. Joanne wanted to impress upon me the sadistic nature of the abuse."

Jesse's hands tightened on the steering wheel. "It's always difficult to accept that side of human nature. I've seen my share of hospital patients who have been victims of violence. Most of them survived with appropriate care."

"Your profession gives you an opportunity to save someone's life. For me it was too late."

"What happened next?"

"We went to her office to discuss the case. The medical summary left me shaken. She asked if I wanted to get a cup of coffee. We went down to the cafeteria and talked for nearly an hour about our families. We both needed a break from the intensity of the autopsy."

Jesse filled the temporary void in my narrative. "Sounds like you guys hit it off right away."

"We did. An immediate attraction formed between us. We respected each other for taking a professional approach to our jobs. Joanne was pretty and smart, with a keen insight into forensics and a commitment to do the right thing. She encouraged me to pursue the case, despite the lack of support from my colleagues."

"After a few months of dating, we moved into a small apartment in Hollywood. The rent exceeded what we could reasonably afford, but full of the exuberance of love, ambition, and naivety, we took the plunge. She became pregnant with Josie six months later."

Jesse glanced over. "So Josie was an accident?"

"Joanne was on the pill, but at some point she switched prescriptions and we weren't careful enough during that time. We discussed an abortion, but her conservative parents adamantly opposed it. I considered it a viable option, but Joanne disagreed. As usual, she was right. I proposed to her several days later."

"How did you do it?" Jesse asked.

"I'm pretty traditional. I took her to dinner and presented her with the ring. With her pregnancy there wasn't much time to get creative."

Jesse laughed. "I guess not. Justice of the Peace?"

"No, we had a nice big wedding. My law enforcement brethren threw us an incredible party. Those were good times. We saved for and purchased a house. My fellow officers helped us move in, and their wives or girlfriends delivered cooked meals. We both received best wishes accompanied by advice about how to overcome the great odds against police officers having a successful long-term relationship. I dismissed it as petty envy from those cops jealous of my landing a beautiful woman with such professional potential."

"The two cops I dated were divorced." Jesse nodded. "And Josie?"

I smiled with the memory. "Josie was born on a Saturday in September. I thought that like my father and brother before me, being a cop and starting a family was the correct path in life. Josie's birth brought forth feelings of hope and promise. For a year, I enthusiastically filled the role of loving husband and devoted father before I returned to building a case against Junky.

"So, you've been after this Junky for quite a while."

"I was obsessed; especially after witnessing in the morgue what he had done to those women." I told Jesse how I suspected my fellow officers' role in sabotaging the case against Junky. Paranoia settled in and created an unpleasant atmosphere in the precinct. Despite the ugly atmosphere, my perseverance with the case against Junky and the successful bust of a number of drug dealers resulted in a pay raise. Joanne had received a promotion to a senior level, which contributed to our improved financial situation. She reminded me of this periodically in the hope our increased income would ease my temptation from the "Dark Side."

I considered the case against Junky my big moment, like a nationally televised game against USC with the pro scouts watching. The fixation blinded me to the impact the case had on my family, and although that kind of drive and focus might be admired in collegiate sports, those same attributes made my colleagues nervous. As the evidence of dishonesty among the cops mounted, I doubled my efforts at bringing Junky down to demonstrate my pockets were empty and my conscience clear.

By this time, Josie was four and I started the long days drinking coffee, which became a crutch to make it through the day. A few borrowed cigarettes led to chain-smoking. The nights became dedicated to social drinking in a bar with my fellow officers, at least those who were unaware of my role in the bad karma infiltrating my division.

Ironically, my professional decline came with benefits—the honing of my police instincts and capabilities. I began to model the behavior of my criminal adversaries and occasionally act like them while attempting to discover how Benny and his team operated. I developed a dual personality: an innocent and naïve officer in public, and in private a ruthless investigator intent on building a case against the corruption in the department.

Jesse shook her head. "You were under so much stress. It must have been difficult to be with a partner you knew was a crook."

"It was awkward. Benny became more distant, which he told me was due to domestic troubles at home."

I explained how difficult it was to accept Benny's corruption. Partners are supposed to watch each other's back. At first, I dismissed his excuses like a priest accepts a confession with the assumption the confessor is telling a figment of the truth. As it turned out, he had been seduced into the bed of deception, taking kickbacks to ignore and sometimes even abet prostitution and drug distribution from corporation-like criminals, some of whom represented the Mexican drug cartels.

Benny never confided in me or made an attempt at recruitment. I spoke admiringly about my father and brother who entered law enforcement ahead of me, and how they exemplified the proper conduct of police officers. I wanted to emulate their approach to being a public servant. This discussion must have made Benny's anus pucker up inside his blue uniform as he decided to embark on a contrary career path.

"And you were still trying to nail Junky?"

"No. After realizing the extent of corruption and experiencing the tension of the indictment, my desire to survive replaced the obsession with the case. I dropped my personal inquiries and focused on being a regular cop."

"I can't blame you. You had a family."

"I realized my investigations were putting all of our lives in jeopardy."

"But Joanne stuck with you?"

"She did for a while. My behavior got worse as the pressure increased. Eventually, Joanne found living with me intolerable. She moved to an apartment with Josie, which should have sobered me from my muckraking drunkenness. When the first indictments were handed out, Joanne decided to leave L.A. It was the last straw—whether innocent or not, my association with the scandal had threatened her career by implication."

Jesse placed her hand on my knee. "She shouldn't have left with your daughter."

"She should have discussed it with me. I understood her leaving, but with my life in turmoil, I made no attempt to stop her." I remembered feeling like a kayaker caught in a river whirlpool. I could see the calmer river ahead, but I couldn't extricate myself from the watery vortex. "The indictments and the Internal Affairs investigation probably saved me. The suspension from the force put me at home instead of sitting in a police vehicle, but the relief from the secrecy and fear didn't come overnight. The scandal ended my marriage and started a cold war with my father and brother."

"Why were they so hard on you?"

"It's the curse of being tainted by scandal when you have two family members with unblemished law enforcement records."

"I'm sorry. But I do admire what you did afterward."

"What was that?"

"You got out of there, kicked some bad habits, and tried to turn your life around."

"Yeah, I'm doing a great job. I haven't seen my daughter in over a year. I missed her birthday last year. So any rumors I've turned my life around are greatly exaggerated."

"Your wife won't let you see your daughter?" Jesse's mouth dropped open.

"Joanne's main motive for leaving was to protect Josie. Joanne knows I will come to see Josie when I'm ready."

"Are you ready?"

"Very. Josie's birthday is coming up and I have no intention of missing it."

"Good, I'd like to meet your daughter." The thought of Jesse wanting to meet Josie brought on a warm glow inside me until we hit the Phoenix area and the traffic slowed to a crawl.

CHAPTER 24

Jesse and I drove into the treatment center's half-empty parking lot. Despite her previous enthusiasm, Jesse turned and stared out at the building's front entrance, making no attempt to get out of the car. With her index finger, she nervously flicked the cover of a paperback book she had brought to read.

I touched her arm. "Are you okay?"

She smiled weakly. "I don't know what to expect."

"Sarah's very frail. It's only been a couple of weeks. It will take some time. You're a nurse, you've probably seen worse."

"Yes, but it's different when the patient is my kid sister."

"Go in and celebrate her being alive."

She nodded and squeezed my arm before getting out of the car.

After an introduction to Sal and a few minutes of small talk in the lobby, an aide arrived to escort Jesse into the treatment ward. Sal guided me back to his sterile hospital-like office with its brown desk, gray filing cabinets, and white walls. Pictures of his family lined a short bookcase and added color to the dreary atmosphere. Several diplomas hung on the wall above Sal's head, next to a large color photo of him with John McCain. A drawn black shade covered a small window and prevented the harsh Arizona sunshine from entering.

Sal laughed. "You look a lot better than the last time you were here."

Maybe it was true on the surface, but my inner body wasn't buying it yet. "I had a rough time getting Sarah out of L.A.

"Where was she?"

"In a whorehouse run by a ruthless pimp I tried to bust several times."

"Based on your bruises, he must have been reluctant to give her up."

"He had a couple of his hoods work me over until he learned of my intention."

"Which was?"

"To pay him." I shifted in my chair to relieve the discomfort in my ribs.

"How's she doing?"

Sal leaned forward across his desk. "If you hadn't rescued her she'd probably be dead. Her body was very weak and the drugs were slowly killing her. She's not out of the woods yet. We've got her on some programs to help with the withdrawals. We can expect her to recover her strength with proper nutrition and rest. Of course, the most important thing is to wean her off her drug dependency. She has a rough road ahead. We should keep her for several months."

"I retrieved her, so my job is done. The rest is up to the family. Her parents are divorced, so she wouldn't be returning to a perfect family life."

"Yes, Frank Minor spent several days here. He seemed remorseful. Apparently, there were some unkind words exchanged. He said she would live with her mother in Santa Fe. What about the sister?"

"They seem close, but who knows? Jesse's works as a nurse in Santa Fe."

"Having family support will help her. Like any addiction withdrawal, this will be a lifetime struggle for her. There will be temptations and perhaps relapses." As Sal stared at me, I fidgeted with the cuff of my pants, self-consciousness about my own battle with the trifecta of caffeine, nicotine, and alcohol. Sal didn't know anything about my troubles. Despite being old acquaintances from school, we weren't close friends and I had no desire to burden him with my personal problems. Despite a few stumbles, the promise of having a relationship with Jesse and re-entering my daughter's life had kept me mostly on track.

I thanked Sal again and returned to the reception area to wait for Jesse. She emerged about an hour later, her eyes red with remnant tears. I couldn't imagine what it must be like to see such extreme suffering of a sibling.

I placed my hand on Jesse's shoulder. "Sal's a friend and he'll take good care of her."

Jesse's shoulders slumped. "She looks so frail."

"Give her time to get stronger." With my arm around Jesse's waist, I guided her to the car. "Are you hungry? How about a late lunch?"

She nodded. "I'm starving. "

We ate at an Applebee's near the interstate. Jesse said little during the meal. When I paid the check she became more talkative. "Let's go see your mom."

The statement caught me by surprise. I started to protest, but she fixed me with a reproachful stare. "You're right here."

"We could go to the Desert Museum in Phoenix. It's only ninety-five in the shade today. It will be fun," I countered half-heartedly, suspecting she needed a diversion after the clinic visit. However, a trip down my family's dysfunctional memory lane wasn't likely to provide an antidote for the distress of seeing her sister.

"No, you should go see your mother while you're in town. You told me you were in touch with her. Come on. Do it for me?" Her eyes lit up and she placed her warm hand on my arm.

I hated when women used their sexual appeal to make me cave in like a sinkhole. I had no will to refuse this woman even if it meant spending an uncomfortable afternoon with my parents. She handed me her phone.

My mom answered in her usual cheery voice. "Hi mom." I tapped on the speaker.

"How are you, dear?" She didn't use my name, which meant my dad was in ear shot.

"Fine. I'm in Scottsdale visiting a sick colleague. I was going to stop by with a friend."

"Oh my. I'll need to prepare something. I could make some snacks."

I could picture my mom as her eyes caromed around the kitchen trying to remember if she had anything to bake. "Don't put yourself out, mom. We just ate and we can't stay long. We'll be there in a half hour." I pressed the end button and handed the phone back to Jesse. Her eyes beamed as she caressed my shoulder.

En route to my parent's house, I detoured to my old high school to show Jesse the football complex where I had some stellar Friday nights on the gridiron. We parked on the street and walked over to peer through the chain-link fence at the well-manicured field. On the opposite side of the field, the early afternoon sun glared off the large columns of aluminum bleachers where raucous fans assembled during Friday night home games.

Jesse leaned against the fence. "So, you were a star receiver."

"Until half-way through my senior year when I became quarterback after the starter got injured. I got the job by default since we didn't have a legitimate back-up."

Jesse smiled, "You must have been very popular with the girls."

"It didn't hurt to be a stand-out player on the football team." I told her about losing my virginity as a sophomore to Daisy Kellogg in the rickety old woodshed behind the bleachers. After making out one warm night below the bleachers, she led me to the half-dilapidated refreshment stand, and produced a key for the padlock. As a beguiled youth about to experience intercourse for the first time, I didn't question how she managed to get a key, or how often she had visited this same spot. Inside, she hoisted herself onto the sales counter, lifted her skirt, slid down her panties, and put me inside her. Fortunately, I didn't last long because, as we rocked the walls of the unstable structure, I kept having visions of it collapsing on top of us.

I told my friend Robert Anaya about the sexual encounter, and he just laughed as if it occurred every night. Robert must have squealed to my brother about my dalliance with Daisy, who was neither a selective nor a responsible partner. The next day, Bart walked into my room, slapped me across the head, and handed me a pack of condoms. He always looked out for me, and wanted to make sure I didn't become a parent or catch a communicable disease at 15 years old. Things had really changed since then.

Jesse laughed at my story, but she turned serious. "Enough with the trip down memory lane. You're stalling."

I raised my hands in surrender. "It's that obvious? Okay, let's go, but don't tell me I didn't warn you."

• • •

My parents had a modest three-bedroom, one-story brick house in a community filled with retirees from up north and pensioned former law enforcement personnel. Despite living in an arid climate, the neighborhood residents still insisted on trying to keep a green lawn. The checkerboard of yellow and brown patches of grass suggested they weren't very successful.

My mother's flower boxes, filled with blooming black-eyed susans, sat like sentries along both sides of the driveway as we pulled up to the single-car garage. I knew the 2007 Toyota Corolla was parked inside. My parents didn't like to venture very far from home and, except for church events and an occasional dinner, the car mostly stayed in the garage. Despite not having checked the odometer recently, I could probably have guessed the mileage to within fifty miles.

"When was the last time you were here?" Jesse said, as if reading my thoughts.

The question triggered my guilty feelings. I shrugged. "It's been a few years. Probably at Christmas, when Josie was four." I ignored the urge to get sentimental. Re-entering the life of my daughter would become my family priority and the rift with my father and brother would have to run its course. Imagining my father nestled in his recliner, denying my existence, would only pique my anger and cancel out my remorse.

We sat in the car a few more minutes before she said. "Well, go on."

"Aren't you coming with me?"

"Do you want me to?"

"You dragged me into this, so you don't have any choice. Besides, I'll need someone to watch my back, in case my dad is awake and goes for his cane."

She laughed and appeared to be emerging from her post-clinic visit funk. "You're a well-trained policeman so I think you can handle a cane-wielding geriatric. Besides, he can't possibly hold a grudge this long."

"You don't know my dad. His cop pride sustains him like nectar for a butterfly."

My mom answered the door wearing a floral dress. The pink apron hanging from her neck suggested a post-phone call round of baking had begun. She gasped with joy and hugged me. I introduced her to Jesse who received a cordial greeting. The additional wrinkles in my mom's face made her appear older and her dark hair had turned noticeably grayer. But her broad smile radiated from the doorway.

The aroma of freshly baked cookies greeted us as we entered the house. A television blared in the living room where my father sat with his feet extended in his beige recliner, a cold can of beer resting in the plastic cup-holder. After an injury-shortened twenty-year career with the Phoenix Police Department, George Caldwell spent most of his retirement glued to the TV watching the latest in raunchy talk shows and melodramatic courtroom battles. A cane rested across his lap to remind him of the ricocheted bullet that shattered his fibula.

With a voice tinged with embarrassment, my mom yelled, trying to out-compete the TV. "George, Arch and his friend Jessica are here." My father made no acknowledgement he heard, which prompted an apologetic look from my mother.

We sat and talked at the kitchen table munching on warm, gooey chocolate chip cookies, while my mother filled us in on some distant relatives, many of the names and facial images I had forgotten. She finally got around to my brother, the other cop in the family. He and my nieces and nephews from Mesa visited often. Her emphasis on the last word sounded like she was chastising me, but the estrangement from the family hadn't occurred on my end.

My father never made an appearance. Not even the aroma of the baked cookies could entice him into the kitchen in my presence. The sound of the TV had gotten softer indicating my father, although too proud to welcome his professionally tainted son, was still interested enough to eavesdrop on his conversation. Jesse recounted the story about my heroic efforts to retrieve her sister from a violent pimp in L.A., and like a sports announcer, my mother presented the play by play to my father. "George, did you hear what your son did?" She always had a flare for the dramatic. "He almost got killed saving Jessica's sister." She took my hand while presenting my story.

The visit appeared to have a cathartic effect on Jesse. She smiled through the entire conversation, occasionally laughing at my mom's stories. I forgot about my father in the next room to enjoy this rare moment of contentment. Eventually, my mom's focus switched to Josie. My mom played it coy, not revealing how she obtained such recent and detailed information. She did not admit to knowing where my ex-wife and daughter lived—her true alliances to my ex-wife clearly established. I let it pass.

Jesse wandered into the living room to introduce herself to my father. It didn't take long to measure the effect of her beauty and personality on my father. The sound of the TV faded and they engaged in a friendly hushed conversation.

My mom also seemed taken by Jesse and expressed the obligatory "What a nice girl," to which I replied with a perfunctory, "Yes, she is."

Jesse's presence saved me from my mom's gentle inquiries as to whether Joanne and I might reconcile, as if it was only up to me. My mom's allegiance to Joanne was still strong.

Jesse fixed me with a grin as she returned to the kitchen for another cookie. We said our goodbyes with hugs for my mom and headed toward the front door.

Before leaving, I poked my head into the living room, where my dad still sat transfixed to the TV, the sound returned to a normal volume. "See ya, pop." He nodded, and added a grunt I hoped might be the first step in the thawing of our icy relationship.

Jesse insisted on paying for our stay at a Holiday Inn near the interstate, which relieved me from deciding whether to get one or separate rooms. I removed our bags, nervous as to how she would play it. She apparently compromised by getting a room with double beds—just sleeping in the same room with her would be the closest thing to intimacy I had experienced in some time.

We shared a bottle of chardonnay and talked through dinner. Upon returning to the room, I showered, brushed my teeth, and put on a pair of athletic shorts to sit on the bed with the sports pages. The Raiders were 0 and 5.

Jesse took her turn in the shower and emerged from the bathroom in a fragrant bouquet of soap and shampoo. A single hotel towel hung from her shoulders, doing little to hide her beautiful body. She walked over to where I sat on the bed. I looked up to gauge her intent and to appreciate her beauty as an art critic might study the Mona Lisa.

"You're really beautiful." I stammered, getting aroused at the sight of her.

"Thanks. You're pretty cute yourself. Mind if I join you?" She sensuously pushed my hair back off my forehead.

"I'd be delighted." I flung the newspaper to the floor.

She let the towel drop on the carpet before settling down on the bed beside me. Her hand slid up through the pant leg of my shorts to grip me. I pulled her to me and kissed her passionately. She broke our embrace, and fell on her side to help remove my shorts, before sliding back on top.

I paced myself by gently exploring her entire body. My hands, lips, and tongue subjected her to a coordinated application of touch and taste. The soreness in my ribs was forgotten. My desire for her was the cure for physical and emotional ailments.

I focused on her pleasure, caring little about when or how my own climax arrived. I approached it like having the perfect meal where the bites of food became smaller towards the end to prolong the pleasurable culinary experience. She writhed with delight and when it finally ended, we laid there exhausted, her head resting on my left shoulder. Thoughts of Sarah, Andy's murder, and my family troubles faded away, replaced by the aura of this beautiful woman, with whom, at least at that moment I shared an emotional connection.

The lovemaking left me drained, but not tired. It didn't matter to me why it happened. I wanted the moment to last and not be concerned about the future.

Jesse's breathing had reached the steady cadence of sleep; her short hair fell across her cheek and tickled my chest. I caressed her head; my fingers in slow-motion ran through her soft golden locks. I wanted to remember every detail of this night.

Hours later, I woke as Jesse got up to use the bathroom. I became aware of the air conditioning unit by the window rattling and barely blocking out the sound of some lodgers departing in the early morning darkness. She extinguished the bathroom light. Her tall lithe silhouette glided towards me across the thin hotel carpeting. She settled down at the edge of the bed with a plastic cup of water and we each drank half. She slipped underneath the bed sheet and slid over, her breasts and pubic mound pressed up against me, her warm breath caressing my cheek. I kissed her, getting aroused again as I gathered her still warm body in my arms, determined not to let this golden opportunity go to waste.

We slept late, exhausted from our marathon lovemaking. I wanted to stay in that hotel room forever, afraid to venture back to Albuquerque and break this brief magical spell. We showered together and dressed as check-out time passed.

She took her medication so she could share some of the driving. "You look tired." She had reached over and caressed my cheek. "I'll start driving to give you a chance to catch some sleep in the car."

I nodded. At that point I would have agreed to anything she asked, including a return trip to L.A. to kill Junky and his hoodlums. Still feeling the sensuality from the sex and smelling her fragrance, my confidence soared as we headed east up the ramp to I-10 for our return to Albuquerque.

CHAPTER 25

A week later, Frank Minor called after returning from a visit with Sarah. He filled me in on her progress. Frank suggested I come by the office for lunch to meet his partners. He had repeatedly expressed his gratitude for my efforts and graciously paid all my expenses with no questions asked. He said he thought his company could use my services on a part-time basis. I agreed to lunch the following week after my trip to see my daughter. Getting steady work would be welcome.

Jesse provided no hint of having influenced her father's generosity when I mentioned his offer. Jesse and I had been out a couple of times since the Phoenix trip, but agreed to take things slow. I accepted that condition, but never bought the tortoise and the hare competition scenario when it came to dating. The speed at which a relationship developed seemed to me to have little to do with whether it lasted.

Jesse urged me to see my daughter. Her support meant a lot to me, but the additional encouragement wasn't necessary. I retrieved the envelope Detective Anaya had mailed to me. Inside, a printout contained the name and address of a school in the Las Vegas area. After my rescue of another man's daughter, the time had come to see my daughter on her birthday and attempt to salvage that precious piece of my life.

I booked a flight to Las Vegas and reserved a rental car. Jesse sounded sincere in her disappointment that her work schedule wouldn't allow her to accompany me. Perhaps she saw it as a return favor for my escorting her to Phoenix, or maybe she really cared about meeting my daughter. Her companionship would have been welcome, but ultimately, making the journey solo seemed appropriate.

CHAPTER 26

Las Vegas is more than an asphalt jungle of tall glittering hotels and casinos. It's a city perched on the parched desert floor highlighted by bleached lawns, swimming pools with tepid water, and over two million people, many of them homeless. Joanne and I had made several trips there to visit her sister. It was not one of my favorite places.

After a night in a nearby cheap motel, I drove into Henderson, a suburb of Vegas, where my daughter attended school. The mid-day heat was overpowering when I left the air-conditioned comfort of my car parked four blocks down the road from the elementary school. The neighborhood appeared pleasant and the school relatively new and clean. Joanne had made another good decision regarding our daughter.

My body baked as I strolled past the curb lined with expensive cars towards the main school entrance where a group of mostly women congregated to wait for their children. Being the rare male, I ignored their glances and my own nerves, committed to seeing my daughter on her birthday. Another guy playing Mr. Mom with an infant in a backpack harness nodded to me, as if we shared a common bond. Several female parents gave me furtive glances, I assumed in response to seeing a strange face in front of their kid's school. I understood, having worked numerous child disappearance cases.

The group focused on the front doors as the ringing bell triggered the weekday outpouring of kids, teachers, and a security guard. Josie exited the double doors with another girl, but disappeared behind a mass of adult bodies

I inched closer behind the line of adults working in unison toward their offspring to whisk them away to their waiting cars. Josie and the second girl headed straight for a short woman with dark hair, wearing baggy shorts, a blue t-shirt, and leather sandals. Josie looked adorable in her short pink dress and a sleeveless yellow top decorated with a collage of flowers.

I stood five feet behind the woman who greeted the two girls. Suddenly, after a moment of hesitation, she smiled, and with a sparkle of recognition, she bolted into my arms.

"Daddy." That one word and Josie's tight embrace melted my heart.

"Hi sweetheart." I mumbled into her hair, while bending to plant a kiss on her forehead.

I heard an accusatory voice. "Excuse me. Who are you?"

The woman holding the hand of the other little girl glared at me.

"I'm sorry. I didn't have time to introduce myself. I'm Arch Caldwell, Josie's father." I broke from my daughter's grasp and the woman shook my outstretched right hand as my daughter gripped my left.

"Oh my. I'm Claudia and this is my daughter Samantha. " She launched into an explanation of being Joanne's neighbor and then she stopped not knowing how to proceed. The embarrassing moment passed.

I smiled down at Samantha. "I just wanted to wish Josie a happy birthday." I handed Josie the package containing the Miss Kitty bracelet Jesse had helped me pick out. "I think it's something you'll like."

Josie started to open it, but I put my hand on hers. "Wait until you get home. I just wanted to see you and let you know how much I love you."

"I love you too, daddy. Can you come home with us?"

"Not today." Her disappointed face tore at my heart.

"I'll come back another time," I said without the appropriate conviction. "It looks like you're making a lot of good friends."

Josie nodded. "I'm going over to Sam's house to play."

"That's good." I risked an ad-lib. "Maybe you can come to Albuquerque to visit me."

"Really?" Her face lit up with the possibility. "Is that the capital of New Mexico?"

"No, Santa Fe is the capital, remember? But it's very close to Albuquerque." Like many parents, Joanne and I had fulfilled our patriotic duty by teaching our daughter the fifty states and their capitals.

"Tell your mother I said hello." I thanked Claudia for taking care of Josie, whose clutch on my arm had tightened. I gave her one last hug before Claudia turned toward the street with both girls in tow. Melancholy filled my senses as Claudia's blue Chevy van continued down the street with the sad face of my daughter peering out at me through the side window.

I slinked back to my car. Guilt nearly devoured me for allowing so much time to elapse since I last saw my daughter. My turmoil caused me to get lost searching for the freeway. I pulled the car over to the curb and stared at my arm still expecting to see the desperate clutch of my daughter's tiny hand. When I looked up, a large green sign stood ahead directing me to the airport and my journey home to what seemed an insurmountable distance from my daughter.

CHAPTER 27

"What the hell is wrong with you? You just show up at her school without any warning?"

Joanne's angry voice boomed on the speaker of my cell phone. The sun was setting behind me as I drove home from the Albuquerque airport.

"Hi Joanne. Great to hear from you." I plugged the phone cable into the lighter socket to prevent the battery from dying. While married, I had let my phone battery expire on numerous occasions. In response, Joanne had bought me a number of plugs and adaptors for charging my phone. She insisted I be available in case anything happened to Josie. I promised more than once, but broke the pledge many more times.

"You could have just let me know you were coming and I would have made arrangements. You terrified my neighbor; she thought you were a pedophile."

"Sorry, Jo. I just wanted to see Josie on her birthday and I didn't want to bother you, since you made it clear you didn't want me around."

Silence greeted me on the other end of the line. My ex-wife let out a long breath before her voice changed to an air of civility. "Arch, you know I don't want to keep you from seeing Josie. I just needed some time. You need to be a part of her life."

"I wasn't ready."

"And you are now?"

"I think so."

We began to talk like adults. I provided her with the bad news. "Andy's dead."

Joanne gasped. "Oh my God. How?"

"Shot in the back. We had a breakfast meeting scheduled and he didn't show. I found him at his house."

"Oh, Arch, I'm sorry. Here I was ragging on you."

"I deserved it. Besides you couldn't have known."

"Do they know who killed him?

"Not yet, although I have some theories." I gave her a brief summary of my return to L.A. and my confrontation with Junky.

"He's going to kill you one day, Arch. And Josie will be without her father." Despite that grim thought, Joanne put little anger behind the accusation. Because of her history with the case, she had seen what happened to girls like Sarah who fell under Junky's tight grip.

"You disappeared with Josie."

"I knew you'd find us when you wanted. Just call next time you want to see Josie, so we can arrange something. You have the legal right to see her. She adores you and it would be good for her to spend some time with her father."

I mumbled an 'I'm sorry', which I had done so many times now, my apology had lost meaning. "What about her mother? Does she still adore me?"

"Not nearly as much."

"I didn't think so."

Joanne exhaled. "Look Arch. I know what I did was illegal, but I did it to protect Josie."

"I never doubted your motive. I'll call you in a few weeks about another visit."

"That would be great." She paused. "I've got to go Arch. I'm really sorry about Andy."

I was tempted to cram in a few details about the new me—the part about the healthy diet, nicotine-free lungs, renewed exercise, reduced caffeine consumption, only occasional and absolutely necessary bouts with Jack Daniels, and how these changes had contributed to my enhanced maturity. But Joanne had moved on with her life and if I became consumed by my past mistakes, I might forget to have a future. I promised to visit Josie soon, and meant it.

CHAPTER 28

Jesse, Josie, and I were drifting in a boat on a bright blue lake with big trees growing right out of the water. The trees had large bright green leaves shaped like hearts that shivered in the breeze. I tried to make sense out of how the trees could live rooted in such deep water. Sarah floated in a separate boat, but despite my cries, she continued to drift further away. A rope from her boat dangled on the water surface just beyond my reach. I frantically tried to grab it and pull her back towards us.

I woke up sweating and anxious about Sarah. Barbara had returned home with her a few days earlier to a grand celebration of family and friends. Sarah looked healthy after 45 days in the clinic. Fifteen pounds heavier, color and beauty had returned to her face. She seemed happy and greeted me with an affectionate hug.

Everyone glowed with optimism, especially Jesse who voiced certainty of her sister's complete recovery. Despite the hopeful atmosphere around me, my experience with cruelty and disappointment on the streets of L.A. taught me to keep everything in perspective.

After the party, Jesse and I returned to spend the night at her apartment. I wanted to voice my concerns about Sarah's recovery to ensure the family stayed vigilant in their support. Sal had recommended another month in the clinic, but the family wanted her home. I agreed that the family had been pre-mature in their desire to remove her from a protective environment.

CHAPTER 29

I spent a chilly Monday in November investigating a vacant building near downtown Albuquerque owned by Frank's real estate law firm before returning to my office. There had been reports of squatters and drug dealers using the abandoned structure. With negotiation for the sale of the building was proceeding, Frank wanted me to secure the premises to avoid any liability issues.

I stopped for an hour workout, picked up some Chinese take-out, and headed to my apartment. Frank Minor called as I settled in to watch Monday Night Football.

"Arch, we've got a problem." I assumed he was referring to a real estate issue.

"What's up?"

"It's Sarah. She left Barb's house about three this afternoon and hasn't returned."

"Did she leave a note?"

"No. And she hasn't called. We're all hysterical."

"Does she have access to a car?"

"No, Barb had gone to the studio for a few hours. There was no car for her to use."

"Has anyone tried contacting her friends? Unless she's on foot, someone would have had to pick her up."

"Barb's made a few calls, but Sarah hasn't contacted any of her local friends. Maybe you can call Barb."

"Okay, I'll get back to you."

Barb sounded agitated and it took me a few minutes to get her focused. "How long were you at the gallery?"

"I left after lunch and returned around four."

"Could Sarah have walked somewhere from your house?"

She sighed. "No, I live in the outskirts of Santa Fe. She called someone while I was at the gallery."

"How do you know she called from the house?"

"I don't have a house phone." Barb hesitated. "I left her my cell phone in case she needed to reach me at the gallery. But she didn't take the phone."

"Did you check to see if she made any calls?"

"Yes, there are three calls to two numbers."

"Read me the numbers and times of the calls." She gave me the numbers Sarah called that afternoon. The calls were placed between 1:00 and 1:30 p.m. The second number looked familiar. I scanned my contacts for Joey Marconi. The numbers matched.

"Barb, I need to go."

"You know these guys she called?"

"Yeah, one of them is an Albuquerque drug dealer." I wondered how she knew both numbers belonged to guys. She must have tried the numbers.

"Oh, my God." Barb screeched.

"I've got to find her."

"I'm coming down to Albuquerque to help." Panic filled her voice.

"Barb, listen. It's best you stay at the house in case Sarah returns. I'll call as soon as I have her." The optimism in my voice was meant to convince Barb to stay put. If Sarah was with Marconi and I found them, I didn't want to worry about another person to protect in case things got violent.

I loaded my gun and called Frank to give him an update before heading out the door.

CHAPTER 30

A cold mist fell as I drove the streets searching for Sarah with two stops at Low Spirits, Marconi's favorite hangout. According to the bar staff who knew him, he hadn't been in all night.

The first number Sarah had called belonged to Freddie Martinez. I didn't need to call for confirmation. The scenario was clear. Sarah called Freddie, the man who got her hooked, to score some drugs. He referred her to Marconi, the man responsible for shipping her off to Junky. She might end up back there, or worse, if I didn't find her soon.

I called Burns and gave him the details about Sarah and her possible connection to Marconi. I convinced Burns to issue an all-points-bulletin to cover APD and the County Sheriff's Department. He promised to send a pair of uniforms to Marconi's house to see if Sarah was there. APD had wanted to bust Marconi for years. I offered to help make it a reality.

Burns called back a half-hour later as I arrived at Freddie's house. There had been no answer at Marconi's house, so Burns assigned two cops for surveillance. I parked a couple of blocks down from Freddie's place and walked back to wait. His perimeter fence was easy to scale and I hid behind a large boulder across from his front door. An hour later at about 1:00 a.m., a car approached and headlights swung across the driveway.

I peeked out and saw Freddie exit the car to open the gate. He pulled his car up to the garage. I followed along the fence in the shadows away from the floodlights on the side of the house. The garage door opened automatically at the approach of the car. I crouched by the outside wall of the garage and slipped into the vacant second car spot as Freddie's BMW entered. The garage door closed. Freddie was alone.

As Freddie exited the car, I slid around the car and pinned his slim, tall body between the door and the car.

He jumped. "Jesus Christ. You scared the shit out of me."

"I'm going to do worse if you don't tell me what I want to know, you scumbag." I pressed harder on the door.

"She called me. Wanted to score some coke. That's it, man."

"So, you sent her to Marconi."

"Yeah. It's where I get my stuff."

"He's the one who sold her to a prostitution ring, you asshole."

"I know. I told him to treat her well or I wasn't going to purchase any more merchandise from him."

"Yeah, right Freddie. You're a saint. Better hope nothing bad happens to her. The cops are involved and I'm giving them your name as an accomplice." The overhead garage light had switched off and the car's interior light provided the only illumination. "Open the garage door."

"I can't reach the remote from here. It's in the glove compartment."

"Is there another one?" I pushed harder on the door.

"There's a switch on the wall by the door."

"I want you to very slowly reach into the glove compartment when I release pressure on the door." I pulled out my gun and started to step back away from the car. Suddenly, he lunged forward into the door and knocked me backwards against the garage wall. I grabbed at the wall to catch my balance and briefly grasped a large implement before it gave way. I crashed to the cement floor just behind my loose gun.

In the dim light from the car's interior, I saw Freddie grab a shovel off the wall. He raised it and approached. The car light went out and the garage was plunged in darkness. I rolled and pressed my body under the edge of the car door as a shovel banged into the floor next to my head. Freddie panted above me. I used the car door as leverage against my shoulder and whipped my legs to where Freddie had been standing. I hit him solidly in the back of the legs and felt them buckle. I pitched my whole body around along the floor and swung my legs again. I caught his feet and knocked him further off balance. He fell on his back to the floor and cursed. I headed straight for a small orange emergency light at the base of the door to the house, kicking my gun in the same direction. I pushed in the switch next to the door. The overhead light came on and the garage door opened. Freddie advanced with the shovel in his hands. I reached down to grab my gun off the floor and pointed it at his head. He stopped.

"Really stupid Freddie. Drop the shovel or I'll kill you."

"You're an intruder in my house."

"Go ahead. Call the cops. I have plenty to tell them about you."

He stepped forward, the shovel held menacingly above his head. "It'll be my word against yours. You broke into my house with a gun."

"What difference will it make if you're dead?" I aimed at a spot between his eyes.

He stopped, lowering the shovel. "I just want you off my back."

"I don't want anything to do with you, but the girl's safety is important to me. Look, neither of us is hurt. We can just go our separate ways. Now, drop the shovel."

He turned to the wall and hung the shovel on a large hook. "And the cops?"

"If I find her and she's safe, I won't pursue charges against you for having sex with or distributing cocaine to a minor. As for the cops, you'll have to take your chances with them. Now raise your arms and back slowly out of the garage."

Freddie retreated to stand just beyond the garage door.

"Hold it." My gun was still pointed at his head. "Drop to your stomach, head towards the garage." He complied. With my gun pressed into the small of his back, I patted him down and removed a short knife strapped to his calf. I flung the weapon onto the garage roof.

With my gun still pointed in Freddie's direction, I edged backward, scaled the fence, and returned to my car. I pulled out with a glance back to Freddie's house and started making calls. Neither Frank nor Barb had heard from Sarah. Burns said Marconi hadn't returned to his house, and he didn't answer his phone. I returned to

Low Spirits to find the doors locked. Tired, frustrated, and out of options, I drove home at 2:00 a.m. to catch some troubled sleep.

· · ·

The ringing phone woke me at 5:08 a.m., according to my clock radio. The tone in Detective Burns' gruff voice chilled me to attention. Most of the details raced past. I didn't want to believe. Sarah Minor was dead. With an aching heart, I picked up enough to piece the story together: drug overdose, her body found on the mesa.

Burns said he'd notified the father. I mumbled my thanks and hung up. With sleep out of the question, I stumbled into the living room and poured a fistful of Jack Daniels in to a glass, chased with a glass of orange juice as if that would make it easier to justify a breakfast cocktail.

The ring of my cell phone in the bedroom brought me out of my trance. I raced to it, hoping it was Jesse, only to hear the masculine voice of Frank Minor.

"Arch, I guess you got the bad news?"

"Yes, Frank. I'm so sorry. If only I could have found her first."

"Don't beat yourself up. You did what you could to save her and we're all grateful…" His voice cracked. "I need to go."

"I understand. Let me know if there's anything I can do."

"Thanks."

With the phone still in my hand, I dialed Jesse's number. Her voicemail prompted me to leave a message.

"Jesse. I'm so sorry. Please call me if you need company or want to talk. Call anytime. My thoughts and prayers are with you and your family." I disconnected, my voice sounded hollow and desperate.

CHAPTER 31

Determined to build a case against Marconi and link him to cocaine and human trafficking, I checked the online Bernalillo County records for a list of women busted over the last month. I took the names to the central records office downtown where I compiled a list of blonde Caucasian females booked on soliciting and cocaine possession.

That night, I cruised along Central Avenue near the Albuquerque Fairgrounds scouting for blonde prostitutes. Hookers were scarce, those visible didn't match my target profile.

My search shifted to 4th Street north of downtown and closer to Low Spirits, Marconi's hangout. Several recent arrests had occurred in this neighborhood. After driving up and down 4th Street, I saw a short, thin-framed, curly-haired blonde wearing short-shorts and a white halter top. She walked with a slightly unsteady gait, a movement suggesting a drug habit. I pulled the car up alongside her. She hesitated before acknowledging my presence. She checked around suspiciously before slowly walking over to the car to stick her head in the open window.

"Hi handsome. What can I do for you?"

"Can you get in the car? I'm feeling a bit uncomfortable sitting here with you leaning in to the car window." I shifted in my seat for emphasis.

"Okay babe, but it will cost you twenty just for me to get in the car." Her speech was slurred, her eyes distant. I handed her a twenty dollar bill. She inspected it as if considering whether it might be a fake before stuffing it in her tight denim shorts. She removed her small backpack and slid in. The odor of cheap perfume made my head buzz. I opened another window to get fresh air circulating inside. I didn't see any obvious signs of cocaine or crack use. Her heightened anxiety could have been just an occupational condition.

She smiled and turned in response to my attention focused on her. "You can pull into the parking lot of the Lobo Motel. The cops rarely raid the place."

"Hopefully tonight won't be the exception." At my hesitation, she robotically delivered the directions in short stuttered sentences. I drove around to the side of the motel to avoid the other handful of cars present. It must have been a slow night.

She spit out a wad of mint gum into a piece of paper from her pocket. She smiled "You're pretty cute. You're not a cop, are you?"

"No, I'm a lawyer." Frank's card rested in my shirt pocket in case she needed convincing. But I counted on her being too interested in the money to care who provided it.

"Cool." She still eyed me suspiciously.

I grinned. "What's your name?"

"Dawn, like the crack of dawn. For one hundred dollars I'll let you experience it."

"Pretty clever. But I just wanted to ask you a couple of questions."

"What do you want me to call you?"

"You can call me Frank."

"Sure, Frank. So you want a blow job for fifty dollars?"

"No. Actually I hoped you'd know where I could score some coke. I've got some high class clients coming into town and they like to party."

She laughed. "How do you know I'm not a cop?"

I smiled "Because you just solicited me. Can you help me?"

She got serious again and shook her head. "I don't know. I don't know."

"My clients might want some companionship." I pulled out another twenty-dollar bill. "Could be a great business opportunity for you and a couple of your friends."

She grabbed the bill. "Could be some party. You going to be there?"

"Of course. How can I reach you?"

"Through the motel here. Just ask for Butch. He'll get in touch with me."

"Great, but I still need some coke."

"Yeah, you and me both." She nodded towards the hotel. "Butch can hook you up."

"Well, seems a bit too much business with Butch. Can you give me another supplier?"

She hesitated. "There's a guy I know, sometimes he hangs out at Low Spirits."

"He got a name?"

"He goes by Joey. But you want to be careful with him. You gotta pay him cash up front and he don't mess around. But once he gets to know you everything is cool."

"You've bought from him before?"

"Yeah, he's pretty generous, if you know what I mean?"

"I'm not sure what you mean."

"Well, once he gets to know you, he'll give you some freebies just to keep you as a customer. And he lets you test the stuff out, just to make sure you're getting what you pay for, you know? And some of us blonde girls exchange favors for a few hits."

"He sounds like the guy I need to see." Marconi liked blondes, supplied them with cocaine as special gifts, and if he found them attractive, traded drugs for sex. Circumstantial evidence for sure, but it could prove to be an important link.

I returned Dawn to her "corner" falsely promising to call when my clients arrived in town. She'd made an easy forty dollars and I had a potential witness against Marconi.

At Low Spirits the sound of loud rock music spilled into the street as I opened the door. The cover charge was eight bucks. The billiards room was empty. I searched the remainder of the bar. No sign of Marconi. The male bartender who served me a beer didn't know Marconi. My adrenalin subsided without the prospect of the confrontation. Taking down Marconi would have to wait for another day.

CHAPTER 32

Sarah's funeral occurred three days later on a rare overcast autumn day in New Mexico. The faces were different from Andy's funeral, but they shared the sad expression of those grieving the loss of such a young life. I boiled with disappointment and frustration from being unable to protect her from the world's evils or from herself.

I offered my condolences to the family and hugged Jesse. She slumped in my arms and sobbed softly, before pulling away. I resisted the temptation to hold on.

Barb came over and grasped my hands. "Thanks for what you did. We should have left her in the clinic longer." Barb choked on the last few words. "When she called, Frank drove over and picked her up. She wanted to come home. How could we refuse her?" Tears mixed with mascara slid down her cheeks.

I placed an arm around her. "You couldn't possibly have known."

Barb dabbed at her eyes with some tissues. "You must find the man who is responsible for this."

"I'm cooperating with the police and conducting my own investigation. Can I see your phone? I'd like to re-check those numbers and times of the calls Sarah made." She hesitated, then removed it from her purse and handed it to me. I confirmed from the call history what she had told me on the phone. Both numbers had been called again at 4:15, after Sarah had left the house. I handed the phone back to Barb without mentioning the later calls.

After the funeral, I visited Burns in his office and gave him everything I had about Marconi, including my theory that he provided the cocaine that killed Sarah. I left out the part about Jesse's involvement in helping me link Marconi to Junky. The abridged version of the story identified Freddy as the source of Marconi's name and Marconi of selling the girl to Junky. Andy's phone records revealed he had been in communication with Marconi, who must promised to provide information as to Sarah's location.

Burns gave me an update on the discovery of Sarah's body. On the morning after she disappeared, a group of hikers found her in the dry grass at the edge of the parking lot of Petroglyphs National Park. The coroner gave the time of death at approximately 9:00 p.m. and diagnosed the cause of death as an overdose of cocaine. Burns had also identified Marconi's number from Barb's phone.

Burns seemed satisfied with my explanation, especially since it appeared to wrap up his case, with Marconi as Andy's murderer. He didn't seem perturbed about my search for Marconi and seemed impressed by my apparent courage in confronting Junky. APD would pursue a warrant to search Marconi's house and pick him up for questioning. They'd had his house under surveillance, but Marconi hadn't returned.

"You have a history with this Junky character?" Burns tentatively probed into my past.

"Sure, back in L.A."

"Well, I'm not one to pry into an innocent man's personal business, but his involvement appears related to this case. What can you tell me about him?"

"He's a tough one, and he's protected, if you know what I mean."

"I figured as much." Burns nodded.

"I spent years trying to bust his ass. He's got lucrative businesses. Prostitutes. Drugs."

Burns leaned back in his chair. "And he's paying off some cops. Maybe some other influential people too. You got caught in the middle."

"Yeah, you can say that." I confessed about my duplicitous actions to Jesse, but I wasn't going to share that information with Burns. "Maybe I'll tell you about it one day over a drink."

"I'd like that."

"I still can't believe Andy would let down his guard."

"Well, you knew him pretty well. What's your theory?" Burns arched his eyebrows and leaned forward.

"Andy would have figured out a way to get Sarah back. Perhaps Marconi promised to help or maybe provide evidence against Junky."

"So he let him in the house."

"Right. Andy thought he had a witness to testify, and he might have been willing to let slide Marconi's role in the trafficking in exchange for knowing Sarah's location, and a chance of winning the bigger prize, Junky. Andy alluded to me that he had some promising leads." Of course, the story I provided Burns didn't include my suspicion that something more sinister had transpired. I guessed that Marconi promised to provide evidence that corroborated the material Andy had in the lock box. Marconi, worried about Junky's revenge, figured knocking off Andy would close the loop. Marconi's interrogation would help clarify his motive.

Burns picked up on my story. "So Sarah, wanting a fix, calls Marconi. He supplied the coke and didn't count on her OD."

"Sure. Maybe she told him I bought her from Junky. So he figures why not make a friend and another reliable customer."

"Does she have money to buy drugs?"

"Her mother told me she didn't find any money missing. So without cash, I'm guessing Sarah offered Marconi sex in exchange for the drugs. Marconi's got a thing for young blondes."

Burns exhaled. "The coroner didn't find any signs of intercourse."

"I figured that. Marconi's not stupid. He would have known his DNA could be recovered from her corpse. If he had sex with her, he would have disposed of the body to destroy the evidence. My guess is she overdosed before fulfilling her obligation." It still didn't explain the negligent discarding of her body in such a public place. I shivered at the image of his goons dumping her frail body from the bed of a pick-up truck.

Which gets back to Marconi's two accomplices. They would have been aware of Marconi's strange encounter with me posing as a husband trying to unload his drugged mistress. Despite my disguise, they might provide enough of a description to lead APD back to me, especially if Marconi had described my reaction when he mentioned Junky.

I hoped Marconi's stooges would have enough sense to get lost when he got picked up. They never saw Jesse, but knew of her presence in the vehicle, rented with my credit card. If they could provide a description of the vehicle, the detectives could make another connection to me, and eventually to Jesse. No, Burns didn't need to know about their involvement. If they came forward later, I would have to figure out how to keep Jesse's identity secret.

CHAPTER 33

Sarah Minor's death had provoked a rage inside me and I'd returned to L.A. with vengeance on my mind. DJ had arranged a night off and scored tickets halfway up at mid-court for the Lakers-Bulls game at the Staples Center. My reasons for the visit remained a secret from DJ until after we'd had a chance to relax, drink a few beers, and enjoy a night of basketball. We didn't even care that the Lakers lost by three points. The day gave us a chance to reminisce about college and our current relationship troubles. Jesse was consumed with grief and I hadn't seen her since Sarah's funeral—my calls to her had not been returned. DJ's relationship with his partner had also hit a rough patch.

We met up later with several former UCLA teammates and partied until nearly dawn before DJ and I stumbled back to his Hollywood apartment. As we tried to recover from hangovers at breakfast, I shared my plan with him. Despite the risks, he agreed to everything.

• • •

Two nights later, I slouched low in the front seat of a rental car staked out at the entrance of the Royal Suites Hotel in Redondo Beach. The previous night proved to be a waste of time. Junky and his goons never showed. I decided to give it one more night. Another no-show might have convinced me to return to Albuquerque in one piece. That's what my gut said, but my stomach didn't influence fate and circumstances.

About 11:00 p.m., a black Hummer with tinted windows pulled past me into the parking lot. My cop's intuition kicked in. After several deep breaths, I got out of the car as the Mercedes disappeared around the corner of the building. I checked my gun and slid it back into the belt holster inside my suit jacket. I crossed the short distance from my car and entered the lobby. It was empty and smelled like Lemon Pledge. A staff member carried on a hushed conversation at the front desk phone.

I pushed the button next to the elevator and the car closest to the lobby opened. I stepped inside, hit the number for the sixth floor on the panel, and slipped back out. The doors closed and the elevator made its ascent. I pushed the button again and the second elevator opened. I hit the red stop button and peeked around the corner of the elevator car. When Manny and Junky entered the lobby, I ducked back inside.

Junky entered the elevator first. I placed my arm around his throat and put the gun to his head. His body tensed. "Don't move Junky or I'll blow your brains out."

Manny recovered from my surprise appearance and started for his gun as he entered the elevator.

"Don't even think about it." I hissed. "Junky, tell him to relax. I just have some questions. Nobody has to get hurt."

Junky relaxed and held out his hands with his palms out. Manny's hands dropped reluctantly to his side.

I stared at Manny. "Slowly remove your gun and hand it to me."

Manny hesitated.

"Do it." I spit.

Manny looked at Junky who nodded. Manny extended his hand with the gun rested in his palm.

I took it with my left hand and deposited it into my jacket pocket. "Now back away from the elevator."

Manny took two steps back.

I removed my arm but kept the gun pressed against Junky's neck. "Junky and I are going for a ride to have a chat. Again, I'm just here to get some information. I don't want to hurt anyone." With my left hand, I smacked the stop button and the doors began to close. "Push the sixth floor button, Junky."

He reached over and pressed the button. I backed away from the door and waved the gun to move him to the rear corner of the elevator car.

"Nice to see you again so soon, Arch."

"I wish I could say the same. I've got one question and I want a straight answer."

"Shoot." He hesitated and then laughed. "Probably not the best term to use. Ask your question."

"Did you have Andy killed?"

Junky fixed me with a pensive stare. "No, Arch. I didn't have Andy killed."

"But you know who did."

"I'm not sure. I can tell you the hit didn't come from this area."

"What do you mean?"

Junky shrugged. "I mean someone in your hood took him out. That's about all I know."

"You're sure?"

"I heard through my associates he'd been killed. But I never made inquiries. Scouts honor." He flashed me a peace sign and a smile. I believed him.

We'd reached the 6th floor and I punched the stop button. "I really don't want any trouble, Junky. I just want to find Andy's killer."

"That why you came back?"

"You got it."

"I admire your courage, and loyalty to your friend." He shook his head. "But I'm not responsible for his killing."

"Marconi?"

"I can't give you a name."

"Can't or won't?"

"Both. Wouldn't be good business for me to squeal. You understand."

As much as I loathed the man, his words rang true. I leaned over and pressed the lobby button. He stared at me. "What would you have done if I had said yes."

"I'm not sure."

"If you had shot me, you wouldn't have left this hotel alive."

"I don't want to shoot you, Junky. I just want to see you behind bars where you belong."

He let out a short rumbled laugh. "I like you, Arch. You got integrity. It's probably the only reason you're still breathing. Too bad Mako wasn't around. He woulda loved to see you again."

"Tell him we're even." I waved him over as the elevator approached the lobby. "Assume your position, Junky."

He stepped in front of the doors and I pressed the gun to his back. Manny stood right where we left him.

I looked Manny in the eyes. "Nice and easy. Everything's good. Keep your hands visible."

Junky nodded to Manny who extended his arms out to his sides. I nudged Junky forward with the gun. We eased into the elevator corridor, with Manny leading the way. I slipped around Junky to the open lobby area hiding the gun in my right hand inside the left side of my suit coat.

Junky held his hands up in front of his chest. "I do business here, Arch. I don't want no trouble."

I backed up towards the hotel entrance as a group of boisterous people entered the lobby.

Junky nodded to me. "Go back to Albuquerque, Arch. It ain't healthy for you to be here."

"Is that a threat?"

"Are you a threat to me, Arch? I only threaten people who are. And I want...let's see how did you phrase it? A straight answer."

I smiled and delayed my response as two couples walked passed us to the elevator area. "No." I lied, thinking of all those documents Andy left me. There had to be enough evidence in the paperwork to put Junky in jail.

The sliding doors behind me opened as I approached. Junky and Manny still stood in the middle of the lobby. I turned and slipped through the doors. Seconds later, a red Buick screeched to a stop. I jumped in and the car skidded as we accelerated down Harbor Drive.

DJ turned to me. "You got what you needed?"

"Not exactly."

"No?"

"I got some clarification, which isn't too bad considering the source." I handed him the keys to my rental car.

He took the keys. "We shoulda taken that bastard out."

"It wasn't the right time or place. Junky's time will come."

"I hope so, for your sake."

175

DJ had wanted to go into the hotel with me, but I knew the more people packing, the more likely someone could get jumpy. I accepted the possibility of dying, but this wasn't DJ's fight, despite his loyalty to me. And Junky wouldn't be able to later identify DJ.

It didn't dawn on me until we left the hotel that Junky had tossed me a bone, albeit a small bleached one. Andy's murderer was in Albuquerque. I knew Junky well enough and doubted he would have shared anything if the killer had been an important business associate. More likely, it was someone like Marconi for whom Junky had no further use.

We turned into the parking lot of the Bluewater Grill restaurant. DJ stopped alongside a row of parked cars, but left the car running. We got out and another large black man emerged from behind a white SUV and approached the Buick. He nodded to DJ as we got into the SUV.

The Buick had disappeared as we turned back onto Harbor Drive and headed north to L.A.

CHAPTER 34

After my flight landed in Albuquerque the next morning, I called Burns to provide a summary of my conversation with Junky and offered my assertion of why Marconi was Andy's killer.

Burns didn't let me get very far. "Marconi's body was found last night in a room at the Doubletree."

"What? He's dead?"

"Yeah, you're quick. Probably been dead for a day or two. The do not disturb sign was hanging from the door knob, but eventually housekeeping decided to go in."

"Murdered?"

"Not according to the preliminary field autopsy report. Appears he fell and hit his head on the coffee table. He must have been pretty messed up. We'll know more after the toxicology is completed. Thanks to your heads-up on his nightlife habits, I sent a detective over to Low Spirits to interview a couple of the bartenders. Seems Marconi was last seen there three nights ago with a blonde."

"What a surprise."

Burns gave me the bartenders' names in case I wanted to follow up. He didn't need to twist my arm.

I called the bar. One of those bartenders would be working that evening. I arrived just after the place opened and headed straight to the vacant bar. A few years back having the whole bar to myself would have been a dream come true. I refused a drink from the bartender, Donald Stringer. We chatted as he dried a mug with a dingy cloth.

"I'm a private detective and I'm following up on the Joey Marconi death. I was hoping you could answer a few questions." I slid a fifty across the bar top and he deftly gathered it in, barely pausing his cleaning.

"Sure, I can tell you what I told the police." He seemed receptive, especially since he had probably received his biggest tip of the night.

"It's all I can expect. You were present the night Joey Marconi was last seen?"

Donald nodded. "Sure, I worked the bar that night."

"And Marconi was here."

He nodded and grabbed another mug to dry, so I continued. "Were you the only bartender working?"

"Yeah, it was a slow Wednesday evening, so Judy went home early and I stayed. Of course, it got busy later. I talked this over with Karen, the waitress working that night. She was also interviewed by the cops. Basically we recalled the same thing."

"What do you remember about Marconi that evening?"

"Well, as usual Joey ended up with a woman. She came in early and I served her several glasses of wine."

I interrupted. "What kind of wine?"

He shrugged. "Maybe Chardonnay. I'm don't remember."

"Go on."

"Later as the place filled up, I noticed a couple of men checking her out. One made advances and failed. Joey was playing pool in the back and he must have noticed her. Joey loved the blondes."

I held out the palm of my hand for him to stop. "Straight, curly, short, long?"

"Oh, long straight blonde hair. I almost thought her hair was too nice. It was shiny and slick like maybe she bleached it. You know what I mean?"

"Sure. Could it have been a wig?"

"Now that you mention it. That did cross my mind."

"Did you tell the cops that?"

"I don't recall." He thought for a moment "No, not the part about thinking it was a wig."

"What happened next?"

"So Joey comes over and she seemed to give him the cold shoulder like the others. I didn't hear any conversation details, but while moving around I picked up some of the body language."

"Can you remember anything about her voice?"

"It was pleasant. Nothin' unusual."

"No accent or anything?"

"Not that I could tell, but then again I only talked to her when she ordered the wine."

"What happened next?"

"Well, Joey keeps coming back and I could see him putting on the charm. Eventually it seemed to work because he asked one of the bikers at the bar to move over so he could sit next to her."

"Could you hear any of their conversation?"

"No, the bar stools were all taken and the noise level had increased with the music. He started buying rounds for both of them including a couple shots of tequila."

I looked up and down the bar. "Where were they sitting?"

"At the end of the bar. Then Joey moved them over to one of them high top tables over there." He pointed to a round table near the door.

I glanced over and turned back to him. "Do you remember what she was wearing?"

"A real nice strapless blue dress. Really showed off her figure."

"What about her face?"

"Like I told the cops, it was hard to see details. Her hair also covered part of her face. My overall impression, she was real pretty. They were at the end of the bar and, once Joey sat, she was turned away from me. Then when they moved over to the table, I couldn't really see her and I got busy."

"Okay. Did you see them leave together?"

"No. I didn't see them leave, but Karen did. She's a lesbian so she notices pretty women. She said the woman had a knock-out body. It was nothing unusual. Joey didn't fail very often."

"About what time did they leave?"

Donald picked up a new mug to dry. "It must have been around ten when I noticed they were gone. Karen agreed that was about right. Neither of us bothered to check the time."

"Either of you ever see her in here before?"

"No, not when we were working. We both would have remembered her."

I thanked him and left him with my card. I dialed my ex-wife's number from the car. She didn't seem displeased to hear from me. We made small talk, and she turned the phone over to Josie. I told her I loved her and wished her a good night.

CHAPTER 35

Burns called and gave me an update on Marconi's death. They found him in his hotel room slumped between a couch and a large coffee table, wearing a silk robe. The autopsy confirmed blunt force trauma to the head killed him. A small trace of skin on the coffee table suggested he'd met it head on.

"Any sign he had sex with the woman from the bar?"

Burns shook his head. "Never got that far. Sounds like she was quite the looker. Tough luck."

"No kidding. Anything else from the report?"

"Pretty interesting. The blood work indicated a high level of alcohol and a derivative of GBH."

"What the hell is that?"

"Gamma-hydroxybutyric acid, also known as Liquid X or Liquid Ecstacy."

"The date rape drug?"

"Bingo. You might make a good detective yet, Caldwell."

"So he consumed the drug?"

"Right. It's actually sodium oxybate. Marconi had several prescription bottles of the stuff in his hotel bathroom. A real prince, this guy. We found numerous other drugs, including Rohypnol, another date rape drug, not legal for use in the U.S. He had a small pharmacy in there."

"Must have used those drugs to knock out the girls he transported to Junky." I recalled, how easily Marconi accepted my story that Jesse had been drugged.

"Very likely. Or he drugged women so he could have sex with them."

"Could be. So somebody dropped some in his drink at the bar or hotel." I remembered the bartender's description of the crowded atmosphere. Plenty of opportunities to slip something into a glass.

"Who knows? We're still searching for the mysterious blonde he was last seen with at Low Spirits. We can't rule out someone reversed the tables and slipped him a mickey. It's tough, but not impossible to get this stuff. The urinalysis came up clean, but these chemicals are only detectable for six to twelve hours after ingestion, but up to forty-eight hours in the blood. So, we can only assume he initially consumed the drug while at Low Spirits, based on his condition, time of death, and drug detection limits. But he may have also been given a second dose in the hotel room."

"Would that have knocked him out?"

"The coroner said given Marconi's weight, the concentration of sodium oxybate mixed with the booze should have wiped this guy out for hours. He had an enlarged heart, possibly from a history of cocaine use. This drug can result in bradycardia, which slows the heart. The drug could also trigger dizziness or a loss of reflexes, causing him to fall and whack his head on the coffee table. At least that's the coroner's explanation."

"What's APD's opinion?"

"We're calling it an overdose with cause of death attributed to his collision with the table. There's the mysterious woman from the bar, and the drugs, but we can't prove there's any evidence of foul play."

"Given what he was involved in, Marconi might have made a few enemies."

Burns coughed. "There must be a few of his former women victims around wanting to do him harm."

So you're closing the Marconi case?"

Burns leaned back. "Not yet. There was one unusual thing about the scene."

"What?"

"The glasses. The housekeeper said there were four glasses with the ice bucket, but we found only two unused ones. There were several open bottles of booze, and water in the bucket."

"Someone removed the glasses." I leaned forward. "Marconi's drinking partner?"

"That's what we think."

"So, Marconi gets bombed. Maybe rises too quickly. Collapses. Hits his head on the coffee table. Blonde gets nervous and scrams with the two glasses. Pretty quick thinking."

"That's what we believe. Points to someone more professional. We dusted the place for prints. Not surprising, they were numerous. We're still analyzing and checking on previous occupants. And trying to determine if there are other prints leading us to the woman from Low Spirits assuming she was in the hotel room. If she was a pro, maybe from your buddy Junky, we're unlikely to find anything."

"I thought maybe Junky was covering up his tracks. Marconi kills Andy. Junky takes out Marconi." Despite Junky's admission of not being involved in Andy's death, I couldn't rule it out.

Burns smiled. "You plan on going back to ask him?"

"Not any time soon. Do you have any information on the ballistics report on Andy's murder?"

"Oh, yeah. From the tool marks on the bullet, we identified the weapon as a nine millimeter Beretta. We found one with a silencer among the weapons in Marconi's hotel room. We can't trace the exact serial number, but the type of gun matches and it had been recently fired. It's not conclusive, but he seems to have had the motive to kill Andy, and we know they crossed paths. You agree?"

"Based on the evidence you have, it certainly seems possible Marconi killed Andy."

"Thought you'd agree. Let's have that drink sometime and discuss this Junky character."

"Sounds good. Thanks for the info, Burns."

"See ya, Caldwell." Burns grunted and hung up. As a former cop, I could sympathize with Burn's desire to wrap up Andy's murder investigation as quickly as possible. Despite the circumstantial evidence, having the alleged murderer die made Burns' job easier. No need for an extended trial.

I reviewed the evidence again while finishing my meal. Marconi's death still puzzled me. Certainly, his enlarged heart, continued drug use, and unhealthy lifestyle made him a walking time bomb. Maybe he did drop over and hit his head after overdoing the drugs and booze. I welcomed the scumbag's demise by natural cause or otherwise. He represented one affiliate of Junky's I wouldn't need to deal with someday. But, something didn't feel right.

Upon returning to my office, I called Andy's father and gave him a summary of the case, including Marconi's death and the APD's conclusion he had killed Andy.

"Do you agree with APD's findings?" Pete Lujan had been around long enough not to trust the police.

"Yes, I suspected Marconi was Andy's killer. Marconi must have been nervous when Andy presented evidence of his human trafficking." I explained a bit about Sarah and our sharing the case. "I think Andy leaned on Marconi to provide evidence against those responsible for the prostitution ring." Based on the documents in Andy's lock box, I had further suspicions not shared with Pete Lujan or the police. It wouldn't be the first time I withheld vital information.

After ending the call with Pete Lujan, I did a bit of on-line drug research. I started with Rohypnol, a nasty drug with no color or taste, making it a sure-fire way to drug a woman without her knowledge. Marconi probably obtained an illegal prescription, employed it for incapacitating his female victims for sex or transport to California. Reading the details of the date rape drug GBH nearly made my heart stop. A salt derivative of the drug, marketed as Xyrem, was commonly prescribed to treat cataplexy. Distribution of the drug came through a restricted program requiring patients to enroll. Jesse had a prescription for that medication.

According to the police, Marconi had a prescription bottle of the drug in his hotel room. But I was troubled by the coincidence—Jesse's possession of the drug, the drug derivative being found in Marconi's blood at high levels, and the appearance at the bar of a wine drinking, shapely woman possibly wearing a wig. Jesse knew of Marconi's involvement in Sarah's disappearance from our sting operation. Barb knew Sarah called Marconi before she died and likely shared that information with Jesse.

Jesse still hadn't returned any of my calls. Was she mourning or hiding? I couldn't implicate her unless Burns came up with further evidence. If she had anything to do with Marconi's death, could I turn her in? Perhaps the woman in the bar was just one of Marconi's former victims or a scorned woman. Maybe. Just maybe.

CHAPTER 36

The bombshell exploded the next day as I sat in a tiny safe deposit room at the Duke City Bank scanning the contents of the only unopened envelope of those retrieved from the lock box under Andy's shed. The contents included more testimony, similar to the depositions in the other envelopes. However, the subject material appeared unrelated to the nefarious activities conducted during my time with the LAPD. Instead, this investigation pertained to the illegal sale of weapons in the 2010 trial of Alejandro Mendoza. It puzzled me why Andy would have such transcripts in his possession.

I started shuffling the loose sheets back in order to place them in the envelope when a name jumped off the page, Bart Caldwell. I backtracked to review the last several paragraphs to place into context the sudden appearance of my brother's name in a legal document involving a convicted gun smuggler. The introduction by the stenographer on the preceding page gave my brother's affiliation as the U.S. Bureau of Alcohol, Tobacco, Firearms and Explosives. I had no idea he had left Arizona State to work for the feds. Did my mother know and not tell me?

I read on. My brother had been subpoenaed to testify in the case because the BATFE Phoenix had allowed the transfer of about 100 guns into Mexico despite the objections of U.S. Immigration and Customs Enforcement. The guns were part of a plan to set up the Sinaloa Cartel kingpin, Roberto Rodriguez, nicknamed Rambo. However, the Mexican authorities responsible for arresting Rambo claimed ATF agents who were on the take abetted the kingpin's escape. The tip came from someone in the Bureau. My brother had been questioned. What a revelation. Andy had many reliable contacts, but I never imagined they extended so deeply into the law enforcement community.

On my return home, my hands tightened on the steering wheel. I burned with the urge to confront him. I recalled my brother's condemnation of me even before any evidence had been presented against me and his refusal to acknowledge my acquittal.

The message light on my home phone was blinking as I entered my apartment. Like most family information, my mother delivered the news of my sister-in-law's pregnancy with child number three. Her announcement acted like Pepto-Bismol to calm the rage inside me. Bart's testimony in the case didn't prove his guilt, an assumption I had reached prematurely.

Anxious from the events of the day, I tossed and turned that night. I considered what impact a lengthy federal investigation would have on Bart's wife and kids—my extended family. With my alleged history, any hint of culpability in a criminal case from his second son might kill my father.

I resolved to be there for my brother, but first I had to go see my daughter and settle my own family affairs.

CHAPTER 37

I returned to Albuquerque after spending the weekend in Las Vegas visiting Joanne and Josie. The first night after putting Josie to bed, Joanne and I shared a bottle of wine. Under the influence, I gave Joanne every detail of what happened in L.A.

At first, Joanne said nothing. Then, she described her autopsy and the DNA test on skin she had discovered under a fingernail of the first prostitute found dead in the junkyard three years ago. "You remember her?"

"Of course. How could I forget? Her name was Angela. The autopsy just about made me sick."

"You got pretty pale. It was an endearing quality."

"Thanks. So what did the DNA test show?" I sipped the wine.

"There was a ninety percent match to Benny."

"Benny? You're sure?"

"Statistically at that level, anyway."

My head dropped. "Wow, I knew he was corrupt, but never suspected him of murder. Why didn't you tell me?"

"I wanted to protect you. It's why I took Josie and fled."

"I thought you were escaping from me."

"I knew the evidence would send you on the warpath and get you killed or put Josie in danger. I could have faced our marital problems, but not the threat to Josie." Joanne refilled our wine glasses.

"What happened to the evidence?"

Joanne hesitated. "I flushed it down the toilet and never reported my findings."

"Joanne, you could have lost your job and destroyed your career."

"I know." She gulped the remaining wine in her glass and smiled.

The weekend proved successful. Our confessions unleashed secrets carried around for years. The trip brought hope we could salvage a friendship, despite our loss of love. The rekindled trust between us brought peace of mind and a renewed commitment to raising our daughter together.

CHAPTER 38

Pete Lujan called as I entered my apartment after returning from Las Vegas. "Arch, I just came from Andy's house. APD called and said they had concluded their investigation so I went over there to clean up and found the place ransacked."

A chill radiated down my spine. Whoever plundered the house was likely interested in what I now possessed. Could they know about the documents in the lock box? Someone now had a motive to kill me. "Probably Marconi's business partners trying to find any other evidence Andy might have possessed."

"Do you know who these people are?"

"I have some theories. Did you report it to the police?"

"Yes, I contacted that detective you mentioned. Burns."

"Good." The possibility of Junky's boys lurking around Albuquerque brought me no comfort. "I'll keep you updated."

"Thanks, Arch. Let me know if I can help."

"I will Mr. Lujan."

I drove to the bank to retrieve the envelopes from the safe deposit box, except for the one containing my brother's testimony. It was time to grow up, but I didn't want to age too fast. I placed the envelopes in a briefcase and returned to my office. I locked my gun in the safe, and retrieved the business card of an important contact, courtesy of my deceased friend.

I stepped out of my office building onto the street, fearful of a bullet from a rooftop sniper or from a passing car. It didn't come.

At the diner, I stepped behind the counter to the kitchen doorway and paid Bud several months' rent in a cash-filled envelope. My workload had increased—the consequence of losing my main competitor to a murder combined with work provided through Frank Minor's firm.

"Business going well, Arch?" With his left hand, Bud slipped the envelope into his top apron pocket while his right hand whipped a spatula with a rapid metallic clanking at a mass of scrambled eggs and ham on the grill surface.

"About as well as can be expected, Bud. Lots of people with problems these days."

After several loud scrapes across the grill, Bud scooped up the eggs onto a white plastic plate, slid it onto the window ledge in front of him, and dinged a bell. "Yep, don't I know it. You stay out of trouble, Arch."

"Will do, Bud."

I sat a few stools down at the counter craving a piece of their always-fresh apple pie, the one really tempting thin on the menu. Justine greeted me with a big smile.

"Hey hon. Need a coffee?" She placed a glass of ice water in the vacant spot in front of me.

"No Justine. Just a slice of pie with a scoop of ice cream. I'm all about happy food today."

"Why the frown, Arch?" She made one of her own, which didn't brighten up my day.

"Girl trouble."

"Ooooh. Who is she?" She leaned on the counter, chin in hand.

"Just someone I met."

"Is she special?"

I sighed. "Yeah, you could say that. Maybe unusual is the right word."

"Sounds like you really like her. What's the problem?"

"I'm not sure. She seems to be having second thoughts about us."

She straightened and tugged down her uniform. "Well, she'd be stupid not to hang on to you, Arch."

"Thanks Justine. Some things are beyond our control."

"You hang in there, Arch. Things happen for a reason. Hopefully everything will work out."

"We'll see."

She returned with a plate full of heated pie, the melting ice cream oozing down the sides and pooling on the plate. "I got you the last piece with an extra portion. You look like you need it."

"Just what the doctor ordered." I dug in.

After finishing the pie, I left her a big tip on the counter for the pep talk. The sugar rush was free.

Bud's wife was absent from her perch at the front door, so I asked her replacement, a young, spindly, bespectacled college student, to call a cab for me. I retreated away from the restaurant window, and waited, briefcase in hand.

When the cab arrived, I slipped into the back seat and gave the address to the driver. Fifteen minutes later, we pulled into a visitor's parking lot. Conflicting emotions hit me. The desire to do the right thing compelled me to continue, whatever the consequences.

I inhaled deeply, paid the fare, and exited the cab. I walked to the front of the red brick guardhouse to check in. My watch said 11:23 a.m. Perhaps being early would earn me some points.

A tall, clean-shaven man wearing shades and a dark suit arrived to escort me into the building. He waved his card in front of a small sensor box and we entered through a black iron gate in the fence. I stopped, gazed up at the American, New Mexico, and F.B.I. flags, stiff in the desert breeze, and strode with my precious papers through the front door

ABOUT THE AUTHOR

Pete David is an environmental consultant living with his wife, Carolyn, in the foothills of the Sandia Mountains of Albuquerque, New Mexico. L.A. Confrontational is his second novel. For more information visit his website at www.petedavidbooks.com.

www.ingramcontent.com/pod-product-compliance
Lightning Source LLC
Chambersburg PA
CBHW070021260626
47159CB00005B/1913